UNFORGETTABLE

J.P. BOWIE

Unforgettable
ISBN # 978-1-80250-950-2
©Copyright J.P. Bowie 2022
Cover Art by Kelly Martin ©Copyright May 2022
Interior text design by Claire Siemaszkiewicz
Pride Publishing

Teaching the Cowboy
Loving the Cowboy
Naming the Cowboy

My Vampire and I
My Vampire and I
My Vampire Lover
Duet in Blood
Blood Resurrection
Bound in Blood
Blood Lure
Blood Lust
Blood Talisman
Blood Vigilance
Blood Kiss

Anthologies
Fabulous Brits: Under the Law
Naughty Nooners: Lunches in Laguna
Friction: Cruising
Saddle Up 'N' Ride: Ride 'em Hard Cowboy
Promoted by the Billionaire: Fly to Him
Heatwave: Summer Bliss

Collections
Christmas Spirits: A Present Christmas
Homecoming: Blueprint for Love
Yule Be Mine: A Special Christmas
Immortal Love: Night Wing
A Little Bit Cupid: Valentine's Day Blues
My Bloody Valentine: Dark Valentine

UNFORGETTABLE

Dedication

Thanks again to Claire Siemaszkiewicz and Rebecca Scott at Pride Publishing for their continued support. And to my editor Rebecca Baker for her keen insight into what makes my books better — thank you!
Thanks also to Phil for putting up with me for nigh on twenty-eight years! Love you!

Chapter One

Blake had never been one for art shows and, unlike a lot of gay guys, not that much into musicals either. So why he was peering into the window of an art gallery in downtown LA showcasing the work of one Alexander Martin was a bit of a mystery. For a long moment he stood gazing at the display of a black-and-white photograph featuring a rocky seashore, boiling surf surging under a cliff wall.

Nice, he thought at first glance. *A bit Ansel Adams.* The major difference being when he stared at the photograph more closely, the subtle outline of a naked man reached out as if to touch the waves.

"Beautiful..."

His murmured comment must have caught the attention of a woman standing a few feet away from him. She smiled then gave him a flirty look. "Takes one to know one, I guess," she said.

"Sorry?"

"You know what I mean." She opened the door to the gallery and held it for Blake, probably amused at his flaming cheeks while she gazed without any sign of embarrassment at him, again with the flirting. "Don't tell me you don't know how good-looking you are, sweetie."

Blake stared at her, slightly amazed at how bold she was, and now that they were almost toe to toe, he could tell she might just be old enough to be his mother.

She patted his shoulder. "Alexander Martin's exhibition is to the right, down the hall there," she said. "It's a private showing today, but go ahead. I'm sure he won't mind. Enjoy."

"Thanks," Blake mumbled then added, "You seem to know your way around the place."

She smiled. "I should. I come here every time they have a new exhibition." She held out her hand. "Doreen Leslie."

"Blake Carson." He shook her hand. He was so bad at this kind of thing. Give him a courtroom floor and he was at home, but talking to strangers not so much. *Socially inept*, his last boyfriend had called him. "N-nice meeting you."

"You too, honey. Now go enjoy Alexander Martin's work."

With that, she turned on her very high heels and walked quickly away. Still a little surprised by her overt friendliness, Blake watched until she disappeared through a frosted glass doorway with some gold lettering on it. He had to admit it was nice to stand in the gallery's cooler air. It was September, and the usual California warmth had turned a trifle sticky mid-month.

Alexander Martin... He used to know a boy called Alexander Martin, except he'd known him as Alex. They'd been best buds—more than that really—but that had been many years ago and there was no way this could be any more than mere coincidence. *Right?* The Alex he'd known had never shown any interest in photography—at least not that he could remember—and this work lining the gallery walls was, even to Blake's plebian eye, pretty spectacular.

He glanced down at the brochure in his hand. There was a picture of the artist, and although there was a resemblance to his boyhood friend, he might be wary of going, 'Wow, reunited after all these years'. If in fact Alexander Martin was anywhere around in the gallery, and they just happened to bump into each other.

Of course, the man in the photo was an adult, a handsome adult without a doubt, but the boy in Blake's memory had been a tow-headed skinny kid with a beaming smile. And now? Blake took a second, closer look at the picture, and there was that smile that stirred something inside him, something warm, a distant memory of a summer's day when he and Alex had gone skinny-dipping together in Baker's Pond.

But that had been in DC, or rather, in Bakerton, a small town outside the city with lots of trees and farms and a swimming hole. Just like they'd done so many times each summer, they'd laughed, cavorted and playfully wrestled in and out of the water—but the day that Alex had kissed Blake, everything had changed.

His lips were cold and wet, but when he pressed his mouth more firmly against Blake's, a definite heat stirred, and not only where their lips were joined. Blake stepped away from him, flustered, looking down at Alex's penis which was twice the size it had been a moment ago—and oh Jesus, so was his. Red- faced and breathing hard, Blake yelled, "Whatcha do that for?"

Alex looked away, his expression one of fear and something else—longing? "Sorry, Blako. I-I'm sorry. I don't know what came over me. Don't tell anyone, will ya? My dad will skin me alive if he found out I like you like that."

Blake stared at him for a long time, unable to voice the words that were spinning through his head. He likes me like that? He wasn't even sure what that meant. Like what?

"Like you want to kiss me?" Blake asked him. "You've never done that before."

"I-I know." He looked at Blake again, shyly this time. "Was it awful?"

"No… Surprising is all." Truth be told, now that Blake had recovered his senses, he had to admit it'd felt…nice.

Blake smiled at the memory of Alex's cute face, the corners of his blue eyes crinkling when he'd smiled back at him that day. He stopped in front of one of the larger framed photographs, a magnificent, almost mystical, view of the Shenandoah Valley.

He knew that view. Long ago, on a road trip through Virginia with his parents, his dad had pulled over so they could get out and enjoy what he'd called God's majesty. Blake had been eighteen and the trip had been a reward for his getting enough passing grades to enter the University of Virginia.

That had been fourteen years ago, and now, staring at and getting lost in Alexander Martin's beautiful photographic landscape, a sudden prickling in the back of his neck made Blake shiver and want to turn around, sure that someone was standing behind him. That feeling was borne out when a smooth, deep voice, close to his ear, murmured, "So, what d'you think?"

"It's beautiful…" He didn't have to turn and look at the man by his side. He was pretty sure he already knew who it was. "Alex," he added.

Alex gripped Blake's arm. "*Blako*, I can't believe it's you. After all these years, and I'd know you anywhere, even the back of your head. Especially the back of your head. Still have all those dark curls. This is a very nice…no, more than nice…it's a fantastic surprise."

Blake grinned. "I was kinda highjacked, but I'm very glad it happened. This…this is all so incredible. You standing here in front of me—and this talent you have, that I knew nothing about. Why did I not know?"

Alex's eyes clouded for a second or two. "It was one of the things that I hoped to share with you, but then…" His smile returned, and he squeezed Blake's arm. "It's so good to see you again. I can't quite believe it."

Blake covered Alex's hand with his and grinned. "I know, I never dreamed when I walked in here that—and, oh wow—!"

Alex had pulled him into a hug that, although startling in its suddenness, felt so right, as if all the years had rolled away, and they were exactly where they should be—in each other's arms.

Alex hadn't changed that much, just added some years—twenty on Blake's quick count—and some muscle. He still had that thick thatch of sandy-blond hair, the blue eyes Blake remembered so well, and when his gaze dropped to his friend's mouth, he couldn't help but admire its pouty fullness. *A mouth made for kissing.*

Alex had been a cute kid, and now as a grown man, in his prime, he was without a doubt, totally gorgeous. He wore a black polo-neck sweater and tight black jeans, all of it designed to enhance his lean, toned physique.

"So…" Blake cleared his throat and, although he didn't want to, stepped back from their hug. He felt a tad dizzy. From the rush of emotion that had enveloped him or the distinct impression he'd been aroused by Alex's hard body, he couldn't tell, but he knew he had to get control before his face got any hotter. He hoped Alex had simply chalked it up to the excitement of their unexpected meeting.

"A-are you free for a coffee or something, or are you going to be busy with your, no doubt, adoring clients?" From the corner of his eye, Blake had taken in a group of men and women, brochures in hand, who were no doubt waiting for Alexander Martin.

He nodded. "If you can wait about a half hour or so, or better still, join us. I'm giving a quick tour and answering some questions for future PR opportunities."

It took Blake a moment to realize his hand was still in Alex's firm hold. No wonder he was breathless. The warmth of his touch was most definitely starting a heat in other parts of Blake's anatomy. Oh yeah, right there in his groin. *Jeez, Carson, get a fucking grip*. Or maybe it was the *grip* that was causing his borderline loss of control.

"Uh, i-if I won't be in the way," he just about managed to stammer.

"You won't. And it's so good to see you, Blako."

"No one calls me that anymore," Blake said without any snark. "I think you were the only one who ever did."

"You mind? I can cut it out if you want me too."

"No, it's okay. Kinda nice hearing it again."

Alex grinned and squeezed Blake's hand before releasing it. "Can't wait to know what you've been doing all these years."

Blake watched him walk over to the group, admiring his athletic build and grace. After shaking hands with the men and women, he engaged them in some small talk that had them all smiling then he turned and beckoned Blake over.

"This is an old friend of mine," he said, putting an arm around Blake's shoulder. "*Blake* Carson. We went to junior high together back in the day. He's going to join us on our tour."

The group gave Blake smiles and nods of acknowledgment, then Alex led them into the main gallery where the bulk of his work was on display. Blake was impressed with the sheer number of framed photographs lining the walls, artfully presented with a single spotlight illuminating each one.

He was also impressed with Alex's charismatic presence while he answered the questions from the group and gave details of where and how some of the photographs had been taken, the type of cameras he used, how he got the lighting just right... *Charming and gorgeous. What a combination, and oh, why did it take us this long to reconnect?*

Scanning the gallery walls, he could tell most of the work was landscapes but there were a few portraits and Blake wandered over to take a look. The one that caught his eye was of a place he'd never forget—the swimming hole he and Alex had enjoyed so many times, where they'd spent almost all their summer days together, and where Alex had kissed him.

He blinked as he stared at the image of a young boy standing with his back to the camera gazing out over the water to the tall trees beyond. He was naked, his perky ass evidence to that fact, and Blake gasped when he recognized himself. The mop of dark, curly hair he'd sported as a kid, unmistakable.

How on earth did Alex manage to secrete a camera on that day without me ever noticing? And manage to take that picture without me knowing what he was doing? All those years ago, and Blake could recall it as if it were only yesterday. Murmurs of appreciation from the group behind him made his face heat up again. *Shit, the second time I've blushed in a half hour!*

"Hope you don't mind," Alex whispered close to his ear, and Blake shivered when his warm breath coasted over his cheek.

"Who's the subject?" a woman in the group asked.

"A friend from school," Alex replied.

"Is it you?" the woman asked, staring at Blake. "Alex said you went to school together."

"I—"

"I had a lot of friends at school," Alex said quickly. "I can't remember who this one is."

Some guy sidled up to Blake and said in a low voice, "Don't think I'd forget anyone with an ass like that."

Blake almost choked. The expression on his face must have alerted Alex that it was time to wrap this up. "So, everyone, thanks for coming today. Y'all have my cards, and I'm up for any podcast or blog interviews you want to do."

Blake watched with relief as Alex shook hands with everyone, and they began to drift off, still gawping at the photographs they passed.

"What did that guy say to you that made you look as if you wanted to slide through the floor?" Alex asked, grinning.

"I'm not usually that much of a prude, but he was kinda ogling my ass and said he'd never forget one like that. Kinda creepy salivating over a twelve-year-old's butt."

Alex grimaced. "That was Charlie Lannigan. He writes for a gay site. I noticed him checking you out. He's cute, but watch out."

"That's okay, I'm not interested."

"Good to know." Alex fixed Blake with a long, loaded look. "So…" He took Blake's hand and led him toward the back of the gallery where there was a small coffee shop Blake hadn't noticed before. "Let's have that cup of coffee and start catching up, shall we?"

"I think you'll have more to tell than me." Blake pressed Alex's hand to his side while they walked. He was still somewhat in disbelief that they had connected again after so long, and so out of the blue. That picture of him at the swimming hole kept popping into his mind along with the memories of the day Alex had kissed him for the first time.

They sat at a table in the almost empty coffee shop. "You said you were highjacked into coming here." Alex quirked an eyebrow. "How'd that happen?"

"Oh, a lady who told me she comes here often ushered me inside. She was uh, pushy, to say the least. Said there was a private showing but to go ahead anyway. She said you wouldn't mind."

Alex laughed. "Was that Doreen Leslie by any chance?"

"It was. You know her?"

"Very well. She's my agent, and she manages the gallery. Doreen was instrumental in getting me this exhibition." He smiled, and Blake's heart stilled for a second or two before quickening in his chest. "I'll have to thank her for sending you in the right direction."

Before Blake could reply, a young woman approached with menus in her hand. "What can I get you, gentlemen?"

"Just coffee for me," Blake said.

Alex nodded. "And for me, but I'll have the turkey, cheddar sandwich, on whole wheat, please. Not hungry, Blake?"

"I had lunch earlier."

"I'll get your coffees right away." The woman left still carrying the menus.

"So..." Alex leaned back in his chair. "Lot of catching up to do, yeah?"

Blake gazed at him, taking in the near male perfection that little Alex Martin had become. "*Lots* to catch up on, Alex. You disappeared on me." He tried to keep the accusatory tone out of his voice, but it was hard, because in Blake's mind, Alex *had* disappeared, and no one seemed to have known where he'd gone.

Alex's eyes clouded for a moment then the trace of a smile lifted his lips. "Must've seemed like that, I guess. Did you miss me?"

"Silly question. Of course, I missed you. You were my best friend. I missed the heck outta you, Alex. I pestered your folks about where you were until they told me to quit bugging them, and when you were home, they'd let me know." Blake sighed. "I asked my mom if she could find out, and she spoke to your folks but they gave her no information, or so she said. She looked mad, but didn't tell me why."

"How is your mom?" Alex asked.

"She died a few years ago. Liver cancer."

"I'm sorry. I remember her being a great lady. So kind to me. She never seemed to mind me being over at your house all the time."

Blake smiled. "She liked you. I used to pretend to pout and say she liked you more than me."

"Well, that's easy to understand," Alex teased.

"Hey." Blake gave him a mock glare.

"And your dad?"

"Gone too." Blake sighed. "Just last year. He had a heart attack. He always said he wanted to go quick, and he did. He was living in LA with me at the time, so it was a shock."

"It must've been. Gee, Blake, I'm so sorry for what you've gone through. I know you were pretty tight with your folks when we were kids."

"We were, they were good parents. Better than most from what I've learned over the years. What about your—?"

"I have no idea." Alex's mouth thinned, his full lips pulled into a tight line.

Blake gaped at him. "Really?"

"Really." He looked up at the busboy who served their coffees. "I was eighteen when I was cut loose," he said after the boy had gone, "and I didn't go back home…ever."

"What d'you mean by 'cut loose'?"

Chapter Two

For several long moments, Alex didn't say anything. He was trying to decide whether to explain what he'd meant or to change the subject. Did he really want to tell Blake what had happened all those years ago? After all, it was water under the bridge now. Nothing would be changed by Blake knowing. It had happened, and it was over with, and he'd moved on long ago, left the bitter hurt and resentment behind, for the most part. Except when the memories would invade his mind while he slept. There was no controlling that.

But meeting Blake again, that same spark he'd experienced being with him when they were twelve years old was back, and how was that even possible? But it was there. He could feel it deep inside him. Twenty years had passed since then...since that first kiss, since that surprised look on Blake's face, since Alex's sudden rush of fear of rebuttal, only to be replaced with warmth when Blake had reached out and kissed his cheek, rubbed their noses together and smiled.

He had loved Blake then, and somehow, despite the odds against it, during the years of their separation, that love had never dissipated, and the evidence of it was in the way his heart beat faster and his skin tingled every time he looked into Blake's hazel eyes.

"Alex?"

"Yeah, sorry, Blake." He focused on the man in front of him, wanting to touch him, ease away the frown of concern on his handsome face. He was slightly taller than Alex. When had that happened? *Broader in the shoulders too...masculine.* Alex couldn't wait to feel that hard, hunky body pressed to his again. *Focus, idiot...*

"You were so deep in thought, and some of them not pleasant ones, from what I could see."

Alex nodded then took a deep sip of his coffee. "You asked what I meant by 'cut me loose'. You've heard of conversion therapy, of course."

"Yeah, but the word *therapy* doesn't really apply."

"You're right. Abuse would be the correct term. Abuse that goes unpunished because parents approve of it. Because the abusers are encouraged in their perverse ways by the very establishments that should protect children from their clutches."

Blake's hand trembled when he raised his coffee cup to his lips. "I can't imagine putting kids through something like that."

"Of course you can't, but my folks could." Alex knew his tone was sharp and angry. And oh shit, he didn't want the conversation to veer into that part of his life, the part he tried so hard to put behind him, thrust into the dark corners of his mind where it could stay, safely out of reach. Until the dead of night, or moments like this.

He sighed. "Damn, I don't want to talk about this right now. It's so good to see you again, Blako." He ran his fingers over the back of Blake's hand. "If we have to talk about the past, I'd rather it was about the times we spent together, the fun we had, the joy I remember in knowing you, being with you. Not the crap that happened later."

"I understand." Blake turned his hand palm upwards to capture Alex's fingers with his own. "But any time you want to tell me, I'll listen. Maybe it would help to get it off your chest."

"Maybe," Alex said, "but not today. Today is for reminiscing about the good times." He sat back again when the busboy delivered his sandwich. "Wow, I forgot how big these things are. Wanna split some of it with me?"

"Just a corner. It looks very good."

Alex cut his sandwich into quarters then pushed his plate nearer Blake. "Help yourself." He studied Blake thoughtfully as they shared the sandwich. "So," he said after a few moments. "You know what I do, but what about you? You look successful…"

"I'm a civil rights attorney," Blake replied.

"Wow, impressive."

"You think so?"

Alex nodded vigorously. "Yeah, I do. What made you choose that field?"

"*Who*, as a matter of fact. My father. He was very vocal about the injustice in the world, how minorities needed someone in their corner. Not that there aren't loads of organizations doing that already, but I wanted to be a part of it. It's not the highest paying kind of law job, but it feels kinda *good*, if you can understand that."

"I can." He reached for Blake's hand. "You know, all those years ago, especially the last year we were together, I knew you were a special guy and I wanted us to be forever in each other's lives. Best friends. I never dreamed we'd be apart for this long." Tears stung his eyes as he gazed at Blake's strong features. "I wish…"

"What do you wish, Alex?"

"That life hadn't been so goddamned cruel, that I could've forgiven my parents for what they did to me, that I could've found you and told you where I'd been and asked you to forgive me for not trying harder to get in touch, and tell you that you meant more to me than anyone else ever could." He grimaced. "Now I'm sounding like a whiner, the last thing you want to hear."

"No, no, you're not sounding like a whiner," Blake assured him. "To be honest, I never dreamed we'd ever be having this conversation sitting across from each other. I've thought about you a lot over the years, wondering what happened to you, why you just kinda disappeared. But now, we have a chance to share what became of us. And, from the looks of things, you've done very well. An artist, and a damned good one."

"Thanks. Your opinion means a lot to me."

A sudden silence fell between them. Alex felt its awkwardness and didn't know how to fix it. Had he said too much, or not enough? Had Blake thought he'd been too open about his feelings and his dislike for his parents?

"Well…uh, I should get back to the office," Blake said, finally.

"Oh, yeah, of course. You're working, sorry."

"We should have dinner, or a drink if you prefer, sometime."

Alex raised an eyebrow. "*Sometime?*"

"Soon. Sometime soon."

"How about tomorrow night? I'd go for tonight, but I have another gallery tour at seven."

Blake nodded. "Tomorrow night then. Call me, and we can decide on a time and place."

They traded phone numbers then Alex walked Blake to the gallery door. He glanced around before pulling Blake into a hug and laying a light kiss on his cheek.

Blake smiled. "Is it safe to say that the conversion therapy was a failure?"

"A total failure."

"Good."

"See you tomorrow then?"

"Looking forward to it." Blake held him for a moment longer, their faces brushing together, and Alex breathed in Blake's scent. More than anything he wanted this moment to last, but then Blake stepped back and pushed the door open. "Bye, Alex."

"Bye." He watched Blake striding along the street. He'd been an athletic kid, and it was obvious he still maintained a strong, toned body — and yes, he still had that great ass. It had felt so good to be in his arms again, if only for that too brief hug, protected by those wide shoulders, hard and warm, the skin on his cheek smooth and scented with a light cologne…sexy.

Was he crazy to be thinking this way? Twenty years was a long time, and although he hadn't mentioned a relationship or even if he were dating someone, chances were, an attractive man like Blake would've had boyfriends, or even lovers during those years.

Seeing him again after all this time had rekindled strong emotions inside him. He'd thought of Blake so many times during his incarceration. He'd longed for his touch, his kiss. Instinctively he'd known that Blake would have gone to ask his parents where he was. He could imagine the kind of reception he'd have gotten and the lies his father would have told him. He cursed himself for not doing more to find Blake when he'd at last walked away from Farmton Manor fourteen years ago.

He'd gone to Blake's house, but a neighbor had told him the Carson family had moved two years prior, and no, she didn't know where they'd gone. Social media had been in its infancy back then, so there had been no Facebook to even attempt to trace him through. That, and the fact he'd had to start making a new life for himself, find somewhere to live, seek out those who could help him with what he wanted to do…professional photography.

The *somewhere to live* had proved easy enough. His Aunt Katherine, the one member of his family that had kept in touch with him for the five years he'd been a prisoner, had told him to come to her when he either escaped or was released. Her warmth and caring had gone a long way to help him rehabilitate after the horrors of forced conversion therapy. She had been the one who'd confronted his 'keepers', demanding to see him, talk to him, know that he was all right. He hadn't been able to see her, but he'd heard her fierceness as she'd berated the men who kept her from him.

Of course they were able to produce all the legal documents signed by his parents giving them full control of Alex's therapy and their permission to hold him at the manor for however long the 'cure' took, or until he was eighteen. She had called him on the one phone call per month he was allowed.

"I told your mother and father exactly what I thought of them, and that I would appeal to our congressman for your release as soon as possible, but I'm afraid, my dear, that all my ranting has fallen on deaf ears." He could hear the tears in her voice. *"I can't believe people can be so wicked, Alex. I will never speak to your parents again, and remember, you will always be welcome here with me."*

Even now, that memory was enough to make him choke back anger and tears. His aunt had been his pillar of strength in those early days after he'd walked free. She had moved from Bakerton to Richmond, Virginia because in her words, she'd never have to worry about running into his parents in the supermarket.

"Maybe a bit of an over-the-top move," she'd told him on one of her calls, *"but you won't have to worry about that either when you come stay with me."*

Alex walked back into the gallery, going straight over to the photograph of Blake standing at the edge of the swimming hole. By rights, it shouldn't exist. The day after his parents had left him at Farmton Manor, they had cleaned out his room, determined to burn his 'sin' from their lives by making a bonfire of his books, photographs and the posters that had lined his bedroom walls. Only his Aunt Katherine's intervention had saved some of his photographs.

She'd told him she'd arrived at his home ready to do battle with her brother and sister-in-law and had been horrified to see them throwing Alex's possessions onto a fire in their backyard. His father had waved some photographs at her, telling her they were filthy and an abomination in the eyes of the Lord. She'd grabbed the photos from his hand and had made off with them after telling his parents just what she thought of them.

She'd kept those photographs safe and returned them to Alex when he came to stay with her. They'd cried together, and Alex had determined that his love of photography, so long stifled during the years at the manor, would now be his career goal. With Katherine's support he'd applied for entry and been accepted at VCU where he'd been very much at home in their photography department. The one of Blake he'd cleaned and enlarged so that it was fit for display.

His cell phone chirping in his pocket interrupted his reminiscing. Checking the screen, he was surprised and pleased to see Blake's name. "Hi."

"Hi, I was just checking to make sure you gave me the right number."

"Oh ye of little faith," Alex said, trying not to laugh

"I really enjoyed our time together." Blake's voice held a hint of shyness.

"I did too. Best thing that's happened in a long time. For me, anyway."

"Me too. Just sorry I had to up and leave so fast."

"That's okay. I get to see you tomorrow. Hey, I forgot to ask where you studied law."

"University of Virginia."

"Oh my God, Blake. I was at VCU. We were so close. Amazing we didn't run into each other at a bar or restaurant or somewhere public."

"That kinda sucks, doesn't it?" Blake sounded upset. "We could've met sooner."

"Right, but now we have a chance to make up for lost time."

"True..."

"And," Alex said slyly, "I can't wait to hear what you'd have done if we'd met sooner."

A light laugh was followed by, "I think I'll leave that to your very obvious vivid imagination."

"It's vivid all right." He looked at the gallery door as it was swung open, and some people entered. "Gotta go, Blake. Call me tomorrow."

"I will. Bye, Alex."

"Bye. Catch you later."

Chapter Three

Blake could think of nothing else but his amazing reunion with Alex Martin, now Alexander Martin, photographer extraordinaire. Amazing, because had it not been for the pushy lady outside the gallery, Blake would have most likely gone on his way when he'd finished admiring the photograph in the window. And after all these years, again it was amazing that the spark between them was, without a doubt, still there. The memory of that day by the swimming hole had been brought back so powerfully by the image of him, buck-naked, gazing out across the water. He still had to ask Alex how he'd managed to take the picture of him without him knowing.

And when had this interest with photography taken hold? Blake couldn't remember ever seeing a camera in Alex's hand. Had he been that unaware of Alex's hobby? He'd been aware of so many other facets of Alex's life, mostly those that had come more sharply into focus after that first brief kiss. A kiss they had repeated over and over whenever they'd been alone together. A kiss that had led to so much more exploration of the delights they had found with each other.

Of course, it had to be their deep dark secret. Alex's parents were not the kindliest of people. Blake himself had felt the sharp end of their tongues when the couple gave their opinions of how rowdy and undisciplined the boys were being, while they played soccer or softball.

It was a marked difference from Blake's father who would join in their games instead of yelling at them to keep the noise down. Blake couldn't imagine living with parents like that, and many times he'd notice a wistful expression on Alex's pretty face when he was at Blake's house.

"Your folks are so nice," he'd told Blake. *"I don't think they'd really mind if they knew how we felt about each other. My dad would beat the crap outta me if he knew we kissed and...you know."*

Blake did know, and after the first time they had gone further than just kissing, he'd thought there was nothing else that could bring him such happiness. Just being with Alex, lying together in their secret place in the woods near the swimming hole, was enough to make Blake feel warm all over, and at night, dream of a life where he and Alex would live together, forever.

Crazy dreams... Blake smiled, remembering those halcyon days when the future had looked so promising, only to be ripped apart a year later, leaving him devastated and alone. His smile turned to a grimace of dislike when he recalled Mr. Martin's forbidding expression the day Blake had knocked on the door and asked for Alex.

"He's not here," Mr. Martin had barked at him. *"And he's not going to be for a long time, so don't come around here looking for him anymore. Understand?"*

"But where is he? Is he sick?"

"Yes, he's damn well sick and until he's better he won't be here. Now go away and don't ask again where he is."

But Blake had asked again, and again, until Mr. Martin had gotten really mad and told Blake if he showed up one more time, he'd call the police on him. Blake had told his mom and dad of his concern that Alex was sick, and that Mr. Martin had said he couldn't ever see him again. His parents had exchanged worried looks, and his mom had said she'd go ask if Alex was okay and when he'd be coming home. Blake could still see that look of angry hurt on his mother's face after she'd spoken with the Martins. She wouldn't tell him what they'd said apart from the fact Alex would be gone for a long time and it was best that Blake didn't bother his folks anymore.

That hadn't sat well with young Blake, and he'd taken to wandering past the Martins' house just in case they'd been lying to him and Alex was there all the time, and he'd be able to see him at his bedroom window. The final blow came when it was announced by their English teacher in class a few days later that Alex Martin wouldn't be returning to Bakerton Junior High. His parents had found him another school that they thought suited Alex better.

Blake was crushed. His best friend, the boy he loved, had just been taken away from him without even the chance to say goodbye to each other, or get his address. He was morose for weeks to the point that his dad had taken him aside and told him he really had to get over the loss of his friend.

"You'll make other friends, Blake, and maybe one day Alex will come back, and you guys can pick up where you left off. But, in the meantime, you have to start learning to smile again…"

Blake sighed. Wow, all those memories he'd thought he'd forgotten, or were just remembrances of a happy time in his youth, were now there at the forefront of his mind. Seeing Alex again had brought it all back, both the good and the bad. The sweetness of their friendship, their shared kisses, their first clumsy attempts at lovemaking before the pain and the emptiness in his heart when Alex had gone away. His parents were dicks, without a doubt, but he couldn't imagine that even they would send their son to a conversion therapy camp. Those vile places were notoriously dangerous and in his capacity of a civil rights attorney, he'd joined with so many organizations intent on having them made illegal.

Alex hadn't wanted to talk about it, and he couldn't blame him for that. It had to have been godawful, traumatizing and something he'd rather forget. But maybe if he talked about it, it might help…maybe. He wasn't sure. He'd offered to listen, but he'd let Alex open up in his own time.

He had to admit that he was really looking forward to seeing Alex again tomorrow night. He'd toyed with the idea of inviting him over to his apartment for a drink and maybe even fixing them both something for dinner. He wasn't a bad cook and he could fix a simple meal of chicken or salmon. It might be more relaxing than going to a restaurant with the distraction of music and chatter.

On the other hand, Alex might feel that a first-time meeting after all these years would be better in a public place in order to avoid any awkwardness of them being alone together. What if things had changed radically between them, and that camaraderie they had so enjoyed when they were boys just wasn't there anymore? It hadn't seemed that way when they'd sat together over coffee, but a whole evening might wear thin after the first hour or so.

Or was he just overthinking the whole thing? He had a tendency to do just that, which had annoyed his last boyfriend, along with his shyness in social situations. Well, Bradford was by far the most critical guy he'd ever met. A bad match from the start, apart from the sex which had been pretty terrific in the beginning, or so Blake had thought anyway. Now he wasn't quite sure what Bradford had ever thought of him. He had run off several points he considered Blake should work on, and when, in his opinion he'd seen no apparent improvement, he'd told Blake goodbye, but not before he'd assailed him with another list of points for Blake to self-improve on.

Almost a year later, Bradford's words could still sting if Blake dwelled on them, although he had to admit life was easier without the constant criticism his ex-boyfriend had been so keen on dishing out. His dad had been so much easier to live with. *Anyway, back to Alex…*

He could bring the option up of either going to a restaurant or inviting him over to his place when they talked about the arrangements they'd left undecided. Then again, he didn't want to put Alex in the position of having to avoid hurting Blake's feelings by opting for a restaurant instead of a cozy night in Blake's apartment.

Oh, for heaven's sake. Stop with all this unnecessary angst. Take the easy way out and agree to anything Alex comes up with. That's it, Blake, let someone else make the decision. God, Bradford was right. I'm hopeless!

* * * *

Doreen Leslie looked around the gallery and smiled. "You did well, Alex, really well. So many people tonight telling me how much they loved your exhibition. Plus quite a few sales, which always makes it worthwhile." They walked together toward the exit.

"Thanks for sending my long-lost friend my way." Alex hugged her arm to his side with affection. "Kinda made my day."

"The super-handsome guy I embarrassed earlier? He was enthralled by the landscape in the window. I knew he'd love your other stuff. A friend of yours? You'd make a very good-looking couple."

Alex grinned. "We were a couple for about a year."

"Oh, what happened?"

"We were kids together, then when we were twelve years old, everything changed for us. They'd call it puppy love, but for me it went deeper than that, and I think for Blake too, but when my dad found out, that was all she wrote."

Doreen knew about his time at Farmton Manor, or as much as he'd revealed to her. Some things just couldn't be told.

"So that was *the* Blake. He told me his name, but I didn't catch on."

"Why would you? There are a lot of Blakes in the world."

"But only this one special Blake." She glanced at him while she locked the gallery doors. "I hope you've made plans to re-connect."

"We have. Tomorrow night as a matter of fact."

"Good. I wish you luck and hope something meaningful comes from it. You, more than anyone else I know, need someone in your life."

"Why d'you say that?"

Doreen sighed. "Because you're brilliant, talented and the sweetest man I know. You have so much to give to the right person, so much to share and be happy with."

"And you think that someone might be Blake? Well, we have a lot to talk about. I don't even know if he's in a relationship or has a boyfriend. That might make things awkward, don't you think?"

"Mmm, maybe." She took his arm as they walked to the taxi rank. "But you'll find that out tomorrow. I'll cross my fingers that he's single and ready to fall in love with you all over again."

Alex hugged Doreen. "That would be the proper story-book ending, for sure." He opened the door of the waiting cab for her. "Okay, I'll see you tomorrow afternoon. G'night, Doreen."

"Goodnight, Alex."

The gallery staying busy most of the night had made it difficult for him to dwell too long on thoughts of meeting Blake again after so many years, but now, in the back of the cab he'd hailed, he was free to remember their special friendship and the love he had fostered for young Blake. A love that had grown stronger during the year they'd been allowed to be together as more than just friends. A love that had been a torment during the time he'd been in Farmton Manor.

Every day and night he'd wondered how Blake was, what he was doing—had he found another boy to replace him? That had hurt most of all. The idea that someone else would be the lucky guy in Blake's affections, that Blake would forget about him as the weeks and months then finally the years, went by.

Even now, the memory of that time made him shudder with rage for what he'd been put through, for what his parents had allowed to happen. His parents, who had never once come to see him or called to ask if he were all right. *Thank God for Aunt Katherine...* His only satisfaction had come less than a year after he'd left Farmton. The place he'd hated so much had been shut down when a new orderly, horrified at the abuse he'd witnessed there, had gone to the police who'd investigated his report, called in social services and had the institution condemned.

Too bad it hadn't happened while he was there, but at least other boys were spared the pain and humiliation he'd lived through for five years. The bitch of it was that none of the 'keepers' had been charged with anything more than misdemeanors, for, just like the newspaper article he'd read about the incident stated, they'd had the full support of the boys' parents.

May they live in shame.

Chapter Four

The gallery proved to be busy the following day, and Alex was hard-pressed to even take a break for a quick sandwich. It was while he was sitting in the coffee shop that he realized he hadn't heard from Blake. He checked his phone for texts or missed calls but came up empty.

"Well, damn," he muttered. *Guess our reunion didn't mean as much to him after all.* He told himself it was okay, but he couldn't totally ignore the frisson of hurt that burrowed itself inside his chest. He'd been so sure they would meet again, that Blake's unresponsiveness was more than just disappointing. It saddened him. The sandwich he'd ordered suddenly tasted dry and unappetizing. Blake had said *he'd* call, right? Not the other way around. Shit, had he said *he'd* get in touch with Blake?

"Oh, for…" Only one way to find out. He scrolled through his contact list then pushed the dial icon next to Blake's name. His call went to voice mail. *Damn.* "Oh hey, Blake, it's Alex. I thought we were going to connect today, but if you're too busy, we can do it another time. Okay? You have my number."

He pushed away from the table and walked back into the gallery, trying to shake off the gloom that had settled over him. *Pull it together*, he told himself. *One missing phone call is not the end of the world.* He forced a smile to his face when a young couple approached him. He could tell they were not buyers, but looked to be full of questions and would prove enough of a distraction for the next few minutes. Maybe help get him out of this mood. As he drew level with them, his cell vibrated in his pocket.

"Sorry, I have to take this," he told the couple when he saw Blake's name flash on the screen. "Be with you in a few. Hi, Blake."

"Alex." Blake sounded out of breath. "I'm sorry I didn't call earlier. It's been a hell of a day. We have a child abuse case going, and the lead attorney was involved in an auto accident and they asked me to step in, and I had to scramble to get his notes off his computer, with his permission of course, and —"

"That's okay, Blake," Alex said quietly. "Take a breath and call me when you have more time. I'll be here until five."

"Oh, okay, will do. Thanks for understanding."

"No problem."

"We still on for tonight?"

"I'm free if you are."

"Good. I'll call you in about an hour."

"Fine, catch you later."

His mood definitely lighter, Alex put his cell away and smiled at the young couple. "Hi, I'm Alexander Martin."

* * * *

Blake sat slumped at his office desk, running through the events of the day that had occurred in the courtroom. Child abuse cases were always hard for him to deal with. His heart had come close to breaking at the sight of the tiny waifs, a boy and two girls who had been victims of their foster parents' cruelty.

After neighbors had reported hearing cries of pain and seeing the kids try to run away on several occasions, the police had finally gone to the house along with social services. The case had been turned over to the firm Blake worked for, but he hadn't met the children until today at the courthouse. Clive Baxter, the appointed attorney, had been slightly injured in a fender bender, and Blake had been assigned to take over.

The children's history read like a horror story. Loren and Emily Johnson's parents had been killed when their apartment went up in flames. They'd died saving their daughters. A year ago, little Joey Carmichael, now four years old, had been found wandering, barely clothed, near a building site in Carson off Interstate 5. One of the workmen had taken him to the nearest police station. When, incredibly, no one had come to claim him, he'd ended in care and after a while fostered, along with Loren and Emily, to the people now charged with their abuse.

It had been obvious to Blake the children were a tight unit. They'd sat close together and held hands while Keren Black, the social worker, talked with Blake and introduced him to the kids. Little Joey had stared at Blake with huge dark green eyes, and when Blake had smiled at him, he'd jumped off his chair and run to him, grabbing his leg and holding on as if for dear life.

"That's nice," Keren had remarked. *"He's usually much shyer. He must know you're a good guy."*

Blake had lifted Joey into his arms and the little guy had played with Blake's curly hair before snuggling against his chest. *"Hey there,"* he'd said softly. *"Everything's gonna be all right."*

"No, it's not." One of the sisters had shaken her head vehemently. *"They'll send us back to that horrible place and they'll beat us even harder because they were found out."*

Her little piping voice had sent a chill through Blake, but at the same time he'd vowed that there was no way would they ever be returned to that abusive couple, even if he had to take them home himself. Which was ridiculous of course. He wasn't in any position to look after three kids, but he'd make sure they were found a much better home to go to.

"No, you won't be going back to those people," Blake had told her. *"We'll find you somewhere with good people who deserve to have such nice kids. Okay?"* The girls had gazed at him with what he hoped was belief while Joey had sighed and fallen asleep in Blake's arms.

The case went the way Blake wanted and expected. The half-hearted defense the defendants' lawyer put up was overwhelmed by the police and social worker's testimonies. Plus, Blake's colleague Clive Baxter had persuaded a couple of neighbors to weigh in. Blake was able to present a damning picture of the foster parents, a scowling pair by the name of Harris, and their despicable behavior. The judge did not show lenience. Following a scathing statement from her they were sentenced to six months in jail, a heavy fine and the understanding that any attempt they made to foster children in future would be immediately denied.

All well and good, Blake thought, but the kids needed a decent home to go to. They'd be put in care until suitable foster or adoptive parents were found. That could take a long time, and Blake wanted to do more for them. It had torn him up when it came time to tell them goodbye. Joey had clung to his leg when he'd set him down, his little face imploring Blake not to leave him.

Why he was so affected by these three, he wasn't certain. He'd seen this kind of scenario play out many times. He wasn't immune to the tear-filled eyes and pinched faces of children let down by the system. He was always left with a hollow feeling in his heart, but this time he couldn't erase the memory of little Joey's big green eyes and the girls' sweet but determined faces from his mind.

"Good job today, Blake." Roger Benson, the senior partner, ducked his head through the partially open door to Blake's office.

"Thanks, Roger. I was just sitting here wishing there was more we could do for all these kids. I never know if they're happy in their new homes."

Roger nodded. "Well, if they don't come our way again, we can be pretty sure they're faring better."

"I suppose…"

"Anyway, good job, and uh, have a good evening."

"Thanks. You too."

Blake sighed then startled when he remembered he had to call Alex before five. He grabbed his cell and punched in the number he'd already put on speed dial. "Hi, Alex, hope you didn't think I'd forgotten you."

"Nah, I know I'm unforgettable." Alex's laughter was rich and warm in Blake's ear. "So, tonight. A bar, a restaurant, or would you like to come over to my place and I'll order pizza?"

Blake chuckled. "So many choices, but I think I'll go for the pizza idea. That way we can relax and talk till we run out of things to say."

"Which may be never what with twenty years of catching up to do. Okay, here's my address. I'm in Pasadena off Lake. You know it?"

"Yeah, pretty much. I have a couple of friends who live out that way."

"Great. Seven okay for you?"

"Perfect. Gives me time to get out of the suit and tie. See you then."

"Bye, Blake."

"Bye." Blake cut the call and told himself to tamp down the surge of excitement that the thrill of seeing Alex again had brought him. Last night he'd dreamed of the man and wished he hadn't. In the dream they'd been making love, which had been incredible, but Blake had awakened, uncomfortably aware that this sleep shorts were soaked and sticky with cum. He couldn't remember the last time he'd had a wet dream. Didn't that only happen to young guys? The dream had been great but in Blake's reality, dreams had a habit of not coming true, so he might just have stymied any chance of him and Alex in bed together, getting down and dirty.

And just how juvenile are you being right now?

It was Friday and the weekend might be perfect if Alex wanted to get together either Saturday or Sunday, or even both days. They did have a lot to talk about, after all. One night wouldn't be enough, and maybe he'd get up enough nerve to ask Alex to stay over at his place and they could have breakfast together and go for a walk in the park near his apartment in Silver Lake. Or they could…

Slow down, ace. You're getting ahead of yourself. Chances are Alex already has plans, so just cool it till you know what they might be. Don't go opening yourself up for rejection.

Once home, he shucked off his clothes, hung up his suit and threw his shirt, socks and briefs in the laundry basket. His place was on the small side, only one bedroom and a tiny den he used as his office. Due to his father's insistence on keeping it clean and tidy when they'd lived together, he still made the effort to keep it that way now that he was on his own. He still missed his dad, a lot. His mom too, although the years since she'd gone allowed him to weather the grief more easily than the raw emotions his father's sudden passing had brought him.

Okay, let's not get morose and go over to Alex's all gloomy and sad.

He walked into the bathroom and turned on the shower. Soaping himself thoroughly with his favorite body wash he wondered what revelations the evening with Alex would bring. He couldn't deny he was hoping that the bond they'd once had might become even stronger with time. He'd felt the spark earlier. *More than just a spark.* The attraction was still there, and he was sure Alex had felt it too.

"Just don't push it, Blake," he muttered. *Go slow. You're good at that. Let him come to you, if he wants to.*

* * * *

The pizza Alex had ordered arrived before Blake showed up, so he turned on the oven to a low heat and shoved the pizza, box and all, inside. He showered quickly then got dressed, choosing to be casual in a pale blue T-shirt and khaki shorts. He hadn't thought to ask what Blake might want to drink so he'd bought a six-pack of Samuel Adams, a bottle of Chardonnay and one of Scotch. He had plenty of water just in case Blake didn't drink alcohol…and he would be driving after all, unless he could convince him to stay over, and wouldn't that depend on how well the evening went?

"*Shit*, I'm rambling to myself," he said aloud. "Why am I nervous anyway? It's not like we haven't met before, like we don't know each other."

But they really didn't know each other, did they? Not the grown-up versions anyway. Not what had been going on in their lives for the past twenty years. Some of that Alex didn't want to touch on, although he knew Blake would be curious, and Blake had always been easy to talk to. Even after all this time apart he'd been reminded of that fact when he'd told Blake about the conversion therapy. It had taken him two years of knowing Doreen before he'd told her, and within minutes he'd spilled about it to Blake. What else would he give away so easily?

He needed a change of mood. "Alexa, play some romantic music, thanks." He listened for a few moments to the sound of lush strings filling the room. He wondered what kind of music Blake liked. Was this too sappy?

A knock at the door had him rushing to answer it. He had to stop for a few seconds to rid himself of the frown he knew was creasing his face into something he was sure was unattractive.

Turn that frown upside down. And where the hell had that come from? *Jeez!* He swung the door open and beamed at Blake. "Hi, glad you could make it!" Shit, did that sound as forced as it had to his own ears?

For a moment Blake looked startled then he grinned as he stepped inside. "Still in salesman mode, I see."

"Sorry, it was a bit OTT." He took the wrapped bottle Blake was handing to him. "Have to admit I'm a bit nervous about this. You know, us getting together kind of thing."

Blake raised an eyebrow. "Really? Cool as a cucumber, I am — not!"

They laughed together then Alex took Blake's arm and led him into the living room. "You look nice," he said, admiring Blake's emerald-green polo. "Green is definitely your color. It brings out the green in the hazel. What did you bring me?"

"Champagne. I figured a little celebration was in order."

"You're right, thank you. It is cause for celebration. Let me get the glasses."

Blake followed him into the kitchen. "Nice place you have." He studied the walls for a few seconds. "Tell me, are you a photographer, young man?"

"Ha ha. How could you tell?"

"Well, either that or you're very keen on Alexander Martin's work."

Alex opened a cabinet and took out two glasses. "You think it's a bit much? Hedonistic, maybe?"

"No, you have the right to be proud of your work. It's amazing." He watched, as after a brief struggle, Alex opened the champagne bottle with a resounding pop.

"Ah, I love that sound," he said, filling the glasses with the bubbling brew. "Well..." He gave Blake a glass, his gaze locked on Blake's hazel eyes. "Here's to us, Blake, and to an evening I never thought I would live long enough to enjoy with you again."

"To us, and to many more evenings like this." Blake brought the glass to his lips for a sip. "Mmm..." He licked his lower lip, and Alex's cock stirred in his briefs at the sensual sight. He leaned in and placed a light kiss on Blake's mouth. This was a test, he knew, and he waited to see how Blake would react.

Blake smiled. "You always were the one to kiss first and ask after."

"How was it?"

"Too soft, too quick if you must know." Blake's voice was low and teasing. "I remember your kisses were longer, more demanding... And you were just a kid."

So this was either the time to press his advantage or take a step back and cool off. Alex didn't want to rush this. Nothing wrong with a little flirtation but jumping on Blake and tearing at his clothes right now might be a mistake. As much as he wanted to get a better taste of those lush lips and inhale more of that spicy scent lingering on Blake's skin, he decided it might be better to wait, some.

He raised his glass again and couldn't help but notice that Blake's hand trembled slightly when he brought his glass up to meet Alex's with a soft clinking sound. Maybe...

"Do I smell something burning?" Blake asked.

"Oh, shit." Alex put down his glass and wrenched the oven door open. He grabbed the pizza box. "Oh, ow! That's hot!" He threw the box onto the counter then flapped his hands about in the air.

"Run the cold water over your fingers, so they don't blister."

"I think they're okay." Alex did a quick examination then started to laugh. "Wow, way to go, Alex. How to impress your long-lost friend in one easy lesson."

"Just as long as you're okay." Blake took Alex's hands in his. "Can't let anything nasty happen to these talented hands."

Alex avoided the obvious innuendo about what he would love to do with 'these talented hands'. Instead, he asked, "One slice or two?"

Blake blinked then grinned. "Two of course."

"For starters, right?" Alex opened the box and made a show of inhaling the aroma of cheese and tomato sauce.

"Right, for starters." Blake eased his ass onto one of the barstools and took the plate Alex offered him. Alex refilled their glasses with the champagne then sat next to him, close enough for their thighs to touch

"Here's to us, again," Alex said, raising his glass to Blake's.

"To us."

Chapter Five

"So..." Blake wiped his mouth on a paper napkin after demolishing his third slice. "That was good." He patted his flat stomach. "Very good, but I'll have to work extra hard at the gym tomorrow. There's something I've been wanting to ask you since I saw you in the gallery."

"Oh yeah? Ask away."

"That picture of me at the swimming hole. How'd you manage to take that without me knowing? Without me even seeing you had a camera tucked away somewhere?"

"Well, you weren't the most observant kid in those days. It was an old camera my grandad gave me, and I carried it in my backpack along with my towel and swim shorts."

"But you never mentioned you were taking photographs."

"No, it was a secret hobby of mine. You have no idea how many shots I took of you. I never asked you to pose or anything like that, just took casual shots of you. It was kinda sneaky, but you made it easy by being so oblivious to what was going on under your nose. My plan was to do a montage of you and surprise you with it on a birthday, or something. Unfortunately, when my father found out about us, he burned almost everything I owned after they sent me away. Plus, he threw the camera in the garbage. If it hadn't been for my Aunt Katherine, the one of you by the swimming hole would have gone up in smoke too."

"Why the heck would he do such a thing?"

"Because he hated what I was. He said I was an abomination in the eyes of the Lord. He and my mother had always been wrapped up in religion, but not the cozy comforting kind. The fire and brimstone, hell and damnation kind. Aunt Katherine caught him in the act of setting fire to everything I'd 'tainted', and grabbed some of the photos from his hand, plus telling him and my mom what she thought of them."

"Good for her. Is she still...uh...?"

"No." Sadness clouded Alex's eyes. "She died two years ago. But at least she lived long enough to see her support for me come to something she could be proud of. She came to my first big exhibition in DC."

"That's great. I remember her. She was a feisty lady."

"She was." Alex gathered up their plates and utensils and put them in the sink. "So now that I have you in my sights again, so to speak, I want to take a lot more photographs of you, with your consent, of course. Maybe..." He waggled his eyebrows. "Some even more risqué than the one by the waterhole?"

Blake shook his head. "I don't think so. My butt isn't what it used to be twenty years ago."

"Your butt is still fine, Blake. I watched you walk away from the gallery, remember? Couldn't take my eyes off it."

"Perv."

"Guilty as charged." Alex took Blake's hand. "Let's go sit on the couch. Like another drink? We finished the champagne, but I have wine, beer or Scotch."

"Thanks, just some water please," Blake said, sinking down onto the comfortable couch. "I have to drive home."

"Why don't you stay over? It's the weekend. We could go for breakfast before I have to go to the gallery."

"Oh, you're working tomorrow?" he asked, accepting the bottle of water Alex handed him.

"An afternoon showing. Doreen expects me to be there, and she's right of course. Only, when we arranged this, I wasn't expecting to have you back in my life." He rubbed Blake's thigh. "Stay, and we can share another drink and talk some more and—"

"Alex." Blake took his hand and kissed it gently. "I'd love to stay with you. Maybe another night when we've had more time to get to know each other again."

"I'm not suggesting we sleep together. I have a guest room."

"Alex." He kept holding Alex's hand. "When you do get to know me better, you'll find that I'm a bit of a slow mover. Something that used to drive Bradford, my ex, nuts. I really do want to see you again, know you all over again, perhaps see if there's a future for us, but I don't want to rush into—"

"You and me having wild monkey sex?"

Blake choked and almost spewed some of the water he'd just filled his mouth with. He gasped and stared wide-eyed at Alex then laughed out loud when Alex looked cross-eyed at him.

"Well, one of us had to get us out of that serious mode we'd just fallen into," Alex said, when they'd both calmed down.

"Oh my God," Blake wheezed. "I haven't laughed like that in so long, I can't remember when it was."

"See? You need me in your life to at least make you laugh." Alex leaned in and kissed Blake's lips. "Stay," he murmured. "No monkey sex, just another glass of wine or whatever, and we can talk some more." He leaned back and smiled, and Blake melted at the sight of those blue, blue eyes he felt he could get lost in.

"Okay," he said, his voice just a tad huskier than usual. "But I'll have to borrow a toothbrush."

"Done. So, a glass of wine to go with the conversation. Or something stronger?"

"I'm good with the water, thanks."

Alex got up off the couch and hurried into the kitchen. Blake sat back and gazed around him at the light gray walls offset by the white trim around the doors and baseboards. It seemed like the perfect background for the many black and white photographs that were interspersed with some color portraits and abstract paintings. One, a portrait of a handsome blond guy, caught his attention. The man was in profile, his face tilted upward as if searching for something, or someone, a haunted faraway expression that sent a shiver down Blake's spine.

"You have quite the amazing art collection," he remarked when Alex appeared carrying a glass of wine.

"Thanks. A lot of years in there." His smile was rueful. "And they're hell when you have to move."

"Who's the blond guy?"

Alex gazed at the portrait Blake had asked about. He sighed. "That's Cody, one of the boys at Farmton Manor—a fancy name for the very unfancy conversion therapy institute."

"He's really striking." Seeing the sadness in Alex's eyes, Blake decided not to push with more questions. He'd let him talk about it in his own time.

"When did you move to LA?" he asked, opting for a quick change of subject.

"Four years ago. It was Doreen's idea." He handed Blake his water and sat beside him. "I met her at one of my exhibitions when she was talent scouting. We hit it off, and she liked my work, so I took the chance, and here I am, hopefully to stay. And you, Blake. What made you move here?"

"I wanted to work for Benson and Sellers. They have one of the best records in civil rights cases, so, like you, I took a chance and asked for an interview during my last year at law school. I started as an intern after graduation. It was rough that first year, but I got a part-time job at night…busboy in an Italian restaurant. It came with a free dinner which meant I didn't starve." He grinned at the memory. "And I roomed with a bunch of guys to share the rent, so it wasn't as rough as it could've been. I'm still friends with a couple of them. One I hooked up with, but I'm not friends with him anymore."

"I imagine that some civil rights cases can be difficult."

Blake nodded. "Yeah, they can be. Like the one I was representing today. It's always rougher when kids are involved, and these kids kinda got to me. They'd been badly abused, two little girls and a boy. Sweet kids.

How anyone could treat them so cruelly is beyond me. No matter how many times we're involved in this kind of case, it just riles me that people apply to be foster parents only for the money it brings in. Not all, of course. There are decent, loving foster families out there too. I'm hoping that the kids I saw today will end up in a loving home." The image of Joey's sad face when he'd said goodbye earlier still haunted him.

"You're upset," Alex said, taking his hand.

"Yeah, guess I am. I even had the wild idea of taking all three of them home with me. Crazy, of course. There can be a long process in fostering or adopting, so I couldn't just make off with them tucked under my arms." His half-hearted laugh held no mirth. "I'd probably have been arrested for kidnapping."

"So, do you like what you do?" Alex asked.

"Oh yeah, I love it most of the time, especially when we can make life better for someone. Not just kids, although, I have to admit that in my mind, they deserve better lives than most. But there are adults out there too who, through no fault of their own, find themselves in shitty situations and get preyed upon by someone stronger, more vindictive. Last week we had this homeless guy beaten up by a bunch of teens who should have known better."

Alex nodded. "There but for providence go you and I."

"But you know better than most what being ill-treated means. Right?"

"Yeah, but I'm over that now."

Blake knew he sounded skeptical. "Really? Years of being deprived of the basics of what life for a young boy means?"

"Blako…"

"Sorry, you said you didn't want to talk about it, and I crossed a line there."

"No, it's okay. You're concerned, and I appreciate that." Alex sighed as if resigned to tell his friend more of his past. "It was hell, Blake, I can tell you that. Something I wouldn't want my worst enemy to go through. Well, maybe my parents." He laughed, but there was no humor in it.

"You don't mean that."

"Oh yes, I do. Along with some of the people that worked there. Not all. A few were nice, but they usually didn't last long. They were either fired for being too lenient, or they quit. One or two went to the authorities, but Farmton Manor had a shitload of influential donors. Twisted individuals who thought it was okay to humiliate young queers and make them see the error of their ways."

Alex threw back the wine in his glass then got off the couch and went into the kitchen. "Like some wine?"

"No, thanks. The water's fine." Blake was still feeling a slight buzz from the champagne, but he was more relaxed than he'd been all day. Alex smiled when he came back and sat beside him again.

"What did you do to survive your time at Farmton?" Blake asked.

Alex grimaced. "I don't know if anyone actually survives something like conversion therapy."

"What are you saying? That it still haunts you?"

"Haunts me?" He took a long swig of his wine before continuing. "I guess that's as good a term as any. I always considered myself to be a pretty optimistic kinda guy, but the creeps that ran Farmton almost managed to beat out of me the hope I held inside."

"Alex," Blake murmured. "I'm so sorry."

"The only people who should apologize to me are the ones who never will—my parents and the men who ran the place. Those who should've known that what they were doing was wrong. Imagine five years of being told you are lower than dirt, an abomination, that you will for sure end up in hell—like what they were doing to me and the other kids there wasn't hell enough. That's what my parents did to me, and why I'll never forgive them.

"I contemplated suicide and tried to go through with it twice, then chickened out. But the second time I didn't feel like a chicken. I felt as if I were giving them the biggest stick up their combined asses, because I was going to live. I wasn't going to let them win by killing myself. I tried to escape three times. Each time I only got to the highway before they found me and dragged me back and tortured me."

"*Tortured* you?"

"Oh, yeah. There is no other word for what they did to me, and some of the other kids, who in their eyes, were backsliders. Electric shock therapy, ice-cold baths, floggings. They tried to humiliate me in such a way that I would have had no self-esteem left, no sense of worth. But I did survive that, Blake. And I think I managed because I would try to help the kids I had grown close to. We weren't allowed to form friendships, but of course, kids will be kids, and clandestine meetings were all the rage." He laughed briefly. "Some of the guys felt it best to toe the line, obey their masters and try to stay out of trouble, and listen to the endless sermons based on their idea of religion and a vengeful God.

"Then there was me, and three other guys. We thought of ourselves as rebels. We went on hunger strikes. No big deal because the food was pretty terrible. The bastards didn't care until one of the guys, Mike, got really sick and passed out. They were worried enough that they had to call in the doctor. Even though he was in their pay, he recommended hospitalization. We never saw Mike again."

Blake gaped at him. "What d'you think happened to him?"

"Nothing like the stuff we conjured up. All kinds of terrible things, some straight out of Stephen King horror movies, but we found out later that the hospital had informed Mike's parents of his condition, and they took him home after the doctors released him. Hopefully they'd seen the error of their ways and loved him enough to overlook his gayness."

"Did your parents ever come see you?"

"Not once, which was fine with me. I don't think I'd have had anything nice to say to them if they'd visited. Nothing they'd want to hear anyway. Two years into that hell, and I hated them more than I thought it was possible to hate anyone. Maybe not very noble of me, but fuck 'em. Katherine was the only one who kept in touch, as much as she could anyway." He smiled. "They censored the letters she sent, and when I got out I asked her what she wrote that they would want to censor. She laughed and told me she called them bastards and shitheads and any other nasty name she could come up with."

Blake grinned. "I remember she had a potty-mouth, even around us kids."

"Yeah, they ended up returning her mail unopened, and she wrote a stinking letter to Ernest Holloway, the head counselor, or Fuck-face as we kids called him,

behind his back, of course. He was a monstrous man."
Alex's eyes clouded, and Blake moved closer to him.

"Is this too much?" he asked. "If you'd rather talk about something else, it's okay."

Alex took Blake's bottle from him and set it, and his glass, onto the table in front of the couch. "What I'd really like, more than anything, is to kiss you again. This time I'm asking first. Can I?"

"Yes," Blake murmured. He slipped an arm around Alex's shoulders and closed the tiny gap between them. He leaned in, and Alex's full, warm lips met his, gently at first then as Blake opened to him and their tongues touched, Alex moaned and fell back onto the couch pillows, dragging Blake down on top of him. The kiss they shared morphed into something much more meaningful. Blake lifted the hem of Alex's T-shirt and slid his hand underneath the cotton fabric, caressing the smooth, warm skin of Alex's torso, lingering over the ridges of his stomach.

"You feel so good," he whispered on Alex's lips. "So hard and smooth...gorgeous." He slid his hand higher and brushed his fingers over Alex's nipples then teased them one by one between his thumb and forefinger. Alex writhed under him, his nipples pebbling from Blake's touch, and he arched his hips against Blake's pelvis. He gripped the back of Blake's neck and held him while he deepened their kiss. Blake pushed his hardening cock against Alex's very obvious arousal.

So much for taking it slow. But this was even more incredible than Blake had imagined it would be. When they'd been boys, what they'd shared had seemed like an adventure, an exploration of each other's bodies that, at first, they'd considered fun, never realizing that it would become an addiction, a need, a love they'd never want to end.

The first time Alex had come all over Blake's chest they'd both gasped from the shock of it. The memory of that moment caused Blake to want to recapture that first time all over again, to feel that same joy on seeing the ecstasy on Alex's face when he spent himself over Blake. He groaned, his mind and body filling with so much lust and desire that it seemed it would overwhelm him.

The strident ring of Blake's cell made them both jump. Blake cursed under his breath but pulled the annoying device from his pocket and glanced at the screen.

Keren Black, the social worker.

"Sorry, Alex, I have to take this." Alex nodded, and Blake turned away while he connected the call. "Hey, Keren, what's up?"

"Blake, I'm so sorry to call at this time of night. I hope I'm not interrupting anything…"

"No, that's okay." Blake threw Alex an apologetic look. "Is something wrong?"

"I'm afraid there is," Keren told him. "The care center just called. Little Joey Carmichael is missing."

Chapter Six

"*Missing?*" Blake had an immediate horrifying vision of the little boy wandering the streets of LA in the dark. The care center wasn't in the best part of town, far from it. All the visceral desire that had filled his mind and body wilted, along with his erection.

"He can't have got out of the building," Keren said quickly. "It's locked up tight after six p.m."

"That's a relief. So he's just hiding somewhere?"

"The staff say they've searched the building high and low, but they just can't find him. I know this isn't something you should be involved in, but Joey kept talking about you. 'The nice man with the curly hair.' I thought if you were there, he might come out from wherever he's hiding. Am I being silly?"

"No, no, of course not." Blake glanced at Alex who was looking at him with concern. "I'll go over there right now and see if I can be of any help. Let them know I'm on my way so they don't call the cops when I come hammering on the door at this time of night."

"I will, and thanks, Blake."

"No problem. I'll talk to you later."

He disconnected the call. "Sorry about that, Alex. I'm afraid I have to leave."

"I gathered that from your end of the call. Anything I can do to help?"

"Thanks, but it's probably best I go on my own. Call you later?"

Alex nodded. "Yeah, we can arrange another night together." He rose from the couch and slipped his arms around Blake's waist. "A kiss for the road?"

* * * *

Blake shook his head ruefully as he drove away from Alex's condo. That ending to their night together had been unexpected all right. He hoped Alex wasn't too pissed off at his leaving. He'd certainly seemed all right when they'd kissed again before he left. The guy could kiss. Blake swore he could still feel the tingle of Alex's lips on his and the sweet pressure of his tongue as it had tussled with Blake's before they'd stepped back from each other, breathing heavily and saying a reluctant goodnight.

The best part had been that they'd gotten on so well. No awkward pauses or questions taken the wrong way. He couldn't help but wonder if Alex's parents hadn't intervened and sent him away, what would have become of their fledging relationship? Would they have gone into adulthood still connected as they'd been when in their teens? Impossible to know really, but it didn't hurt to imagine that they would have kept in touch regardless of different colleges or towns even. And after they'd graduated, what then? Would they

J.P. Bowie

have lived together? Would they have planned the move to LA together?

He remembered what Alex had told him one day when they'd met in their secret place. His expression had been so serious, his voice gentle and husky. "*I'm gonna love you forever, Blake. No matter what occurs, we will always be together.*" How could they have known that vow so tenderly given would become impossible to keep due to Alex's parents' actions? That someone had seen them holding hands while they'd been walking through the woods and had snitched on them to Alex's dad? It was incredible to realize they'd been so close in Virginia without ever knowing that just a few miles had separated them.

Life can be so strange. And what kind of life lies ahead for little Joey Carmichael and the two girls who tried to protect him?

It hurt his heart to think that the kids would end up in yet another foster home, with only the luck of the draw to determine whether it was a loving and caring environment, or miserable like the one they'd tried to run away from. He sighed, wishing there was more he could do to ensure that their future wasn't as bleak as their past.

He pulled up in front of the care center and parked under a streetlight, hoping his car would still be there, undamaged, when he came back. He rang the doorbell, and it was answered by a middle-aged African American woman with graying hair.

"Yes?"

"I'm Blake Carson. Keren Black asked if I'd come over to help look for Joey Carmichael."

"Oh, come on in." She stuck a hand out for him to shake. "Estelle Simmons. This way…" She led him down a long hall.

"Has he been found yet?"

"No, and we've searched the whole place." She stopped at an open doorway. Three women and a young man were seated at a table having what appeared to be cold drinks. "This is Blake Carson, the attorney Keren told us to expect." She rattled off some names, and Blake nodded in acknowledgment.

"Let's get started, shall we?" Blake didn't feel this was the time for niceties.

"We have to be real quiet," Estelle said. "We don't want to wake the other little ones if we can avoid it."

"How many are here right now?"

"Six, including Joey."

"Is there any place you might have missed in your search?"

"Yeah, if he climbed out a window and flew away." The young guy, whose name Blake couldn't recall, smirked at him.

"Well, if he couldn't get out of the building, there has to be somewhere he's still hiding." Blake ignored the guy's snark. "He's a tiny kid, able to slip inside just about any small space."

"Mr. Carson is right, Spencer. We'll just have to go over the whole place again."

"Which room is his?" Blake asked.

"I'll show you." Estelle took him to the staircase, and they climbed to the first floor, Spencer following, humming under his breath. It was obvious the guy thought this was a waste of time.

"He'll most likely come out when he's hungry," he said.

"We can't leave him alone overnight," Blake snapped. "He's been through enough trauma. We need to find him and assure him he's safe here."

Spencer sighed. "Whatever."

Estelle gave him a sharp glare then pushed a door open. "This is Joey's room."

Blake stared at the empty bed then took a quick peek under before opening the closet.

Spencer sighed again. "We *have* checked all of that."

"I'm sure you have and now I'm checking again." Blake brushed past him and stood in the hall, listening. For what, he wasn't sure. A cry, a whimper? The door next to Joey's opened and two sleepy-eyed little girls peered out. Loren and Emily Johnson.

"Hello." Blake smiled at them. "Do you remember me?"

Loren, the older of the two, nodded.

"Have you seen Joey?"

She nodded again and pointed to their room. "He's in here with us."

"You didn't check the other rooms?" Blake asked, astounded that such a simple thing could have been overlooked.

Estelle drew in a startled breath. "Oh, but I didn't want to wake the other children."

"Told ya we should've gone in, especially this one," Spencer said, rolling his eyes.

"Well, at least we know he was with his friends." He smiled at Loren. "Can I go in?"

Loren took his hand. "Yes."

Joey was sitting on one of the beds and flew at Blake when he entered, grabbing his legs like he'd done before and holding on tight. Blake bent to lift him up.

"You had us all worried, Joey," he said. "Are you okay?" He carried the little guy back into the hall.

Joey shook his head vigorously then wrapped his arms around Blake's neck. "I wanna go home with you," he whispered into Blake's ear.

"He's scared," Loren told Blake.

"He has bruises on his back," Estelle said.

"I know. One of the many reasons they were taken from the Harris household, their last foster home." Blake sighed. *What am I going to do now?*

"Well, I can tell he's very fond of you." Estelle smiled. "Do you have children of your own?"

"No, I'm not married."

"That shouldn't stop you," she remarked tartly. "Single men and women can foster or adopt in California."

"Yeah, I know, but I'm not home that much..." He trailed off lamely. *Besides, it would take some time for the authorities to approve me as a foster parent, if then.*

"He's gonna raise a ruckus the minute you walk out the door." Spencer had just confirmed Blake's fear of a Joey meltdown when he took him back to his room.

"Let me talk to him for a little while," Blake said, not sure if he'd be able to calm Joey's mind enough to have him sleep for the rest of the night. He carried the little boy back into the girls' room and sat on the bed. It seemed Joey didn't want to let him go as he clung to him tighter.

"Joey..." Blake tried to keep his voice as low and comforting as he could. "I'm sorry I can't take you home with me, but I promise to come by to see you in the morning. Is that okay?"

Joey whimpered. "Wanna come with you."

"I know." *God, but this kid is tearing my heart out.* "And believe me I want more than anything for you to be happy, but it'll take a little time to find you a nice home. I'll make sure it really is nice and everyone will take care of you. No more smacks, no more yelling. Nothing like that, I promise."

Perhaps he should have had Alex come with him after all. Between them, maybe they could have come up with a plan. But what kind of plan, and what about the girls? It had been his hope that the three of them would be fostered together, adopted later perhaps, but there was no way he could cope with three children. He'd need a much bigger apartment for a start, and a nanny, and… Oh, it was just all too ridiculous to even consider.

Joey sighed, and Blake realized he had fallen asleep. "Can he stay with the girls for tonight?" he asked Estelle, who was standing in the doorway watching them.

Estelle nodded. "Best he does, I think. They seem to get along well together. We'll be arranging temporary foster homes for them tomorrow. Don't worry, Mr. Carson, we'll tell Keren she has to make sure the agencies are extra careful with the background checks."

Blake stood then laid Joey gently on the bed. "Do you share with him?" he asked Emily, the younger of the two girls.

"We all sleep together," Loren told him. We're small, so there's plenty room." She yawned. "Can we have a hug before you go?"

"Of course." He knelt and opened his arms so that they could nestle against his chest. More than anything, they needed love and caring for, and Blake made a vow he would make sure they never had to face the kind of abuse they'd had to endure at the Harris'.

* * * *

On his way home, he called Alex.

"Oh, hi, Blake." Alex sounded pleased to hear from him.

"Hi, just thought I'd call and say goodnight."

"How'd it go at the care center?"

"Okay, eventually. Joey, the youngest of the kids I told you about, was hiding and the staff didn't look in the other rooms for him. The nurse said she didn't want to disturb the children, but there he was, being looked after by the girls. He...he wanted to come home with me, but I told him I'd swing by and see him tomorrow. He fell asleep, so that was a blessing."

"Sounds like he's taken a shine to you."

"Yeah, it looks like it. I promised we'd find a good home for him with caring people. Just hope it pans out okay. I am going to keep tabs on where they end up and their progress."

"Is that part of your job?"

"Not really, but I just feel involved somehow. They are great kids. Anyway..." Blake paused before asking, "See you tomorrow night?"

"I'd like that. We still have a lot of catching up to do and, oh yeah..." Alex chuckled. "You still owe me the rest of your very delectable kisses."

Blake laughed, embarrassed and turned on at the same time. "Were you counting?"

"No, but it seemed like we'd just got started. You're a sweet kisser, Blake, just like I remembered."

"Flatterer."

"You bet, if it gets your lips on mine again. Anyway, I think I told you I have to be at the gallery in the afternoon, so if you meet me there, at, say around six, I'll take you to dinner first—"

"First? What comes next?"

Alex snickered. "You'll just have to wait and see. I'm sure I'll think of something."

"I'm sure you will." Blake was enjoying the easygoing flirty banter. "I can't wait to find out what it is."

"I don't think you'll be disappointed."

"Well"—Blake drawled for effect—"as you said, I'll just have to wait and see."

"Right. Okay, six at the gallery, or come earlier if you don't mind being bored."

"Don't think I'd be bored watching you in action."

Alex let out a pretend shocked gasp. "And you told me you were a slow mover. Were you trying to lull me into a sense of false security, then pounce on me?"

Blake laughed. "Pouncing on you sounds like fun." His cock pulsed inside his briefs. It seemed to think so too.

Alex sighed. "Now, all of a sudden, tomorrow seems a long way off."

"I'd suggest breakfast, but I promised Joey I'd go see him in the morning."

"Ah yes, and I can't possibly be jealous of a four-year-old kid."

"Hope not. See you tomorrow, Alex."

"Looking forward to it."

"Me too. Goodnight."

"G'night, Blake."

Chapter Seven

Alex put his phone down and breathed a sigh of relief. He'd been afraid that maybe he'd scared Blake away with his less-than-subtle moves. That in his car on the way to the care center, Blake had rethought their 'getting cozy' and figured it was too much too soon. But from the relaxed conversation they'd just had, it didn't appear that way. He'd sounded pleased that they'd be seeing each other again tomorrow. With any luck, he'd get to sample some more of Blake's kisses, and maybe, just maybe, they could take it to the next level. It had seemed Blake had been ready for at least some heavy making out before they were interrupted by the call about the missing kid.

Alex would like to get them back on track for more of that. He wanted to keep their time together free of his lousy past. As far as Alex was concerned, he'd said enough, and contrary to popular opinion, talking about it didn't really help. It brought back too many ghastly memories, and although Blake had been sweet and caring while he'd listened, Alex would much rather talk about life *after* Farmton Manor — college, the start of both their careers — the good stuff. It still amazed him that they had both been in such close proximity during their college years and had never once run into each other in a bar or a store.

And now twenty years later, Blake just happened to be passing the gallery where I had my exhibition. What are the chances?

Next to zero, he bet. If he believed in Fate, he'd go with that, and maybe it was. *Life can take some crazy turns at times.* He knew all about that. For the five years he'd been locked up in Farmton, he'd had sex exactly twice, and both times it had been less than fulfilling. God knew he'd been horny, just like any teenaged boy had a right to be, but their keepers had kept a tight lookout for any sign that the boys might get fond of one another, and put a quick, and sometimes brutal, stop to it. The second time he'd been caught giving head, the aches and bruises had taken a long time to fade. As for Cody, his partner, he'd never dared look Alex in the eyes again. There had been no comfort for either of them, only pain and despair.

So it had shaken him when one night a few years later when Farmton was still a bitter memory, he'd seen Cody in a gay bar in Charleston. The shock that had startled him had been mirrored on Cody's face when his eyes had locked on Alex's from the far end of the bar. They'd stared and stared, as if for a long moment neither of them could quite believe their eyes. Then they'd pushed their way through the milling crowd before falling into each other's arms. Alex had tried to fight back the tears he had known were spilling down Cody's cheeks, if his trembling body pressed so hard against Alex's had been any indication of their shared emotions.

"Everybody's lookin' at us," Cody had whispered in Alex's ear after a few moments.

"Let 'em." Alex's voice had been hoarse with emotion. *"Better still, let's get out of here, find somewhere private so we can catch up."*

They'd left the bar and walked and talked for miles, clutching at each other's hands, both of them unable to believe that they'd met again. It had seemed almost impossible.

"So they didn't convert you, I'm guessing," Alex had said wryly.

"No, nor you, judging by where we've just come from."

They'd laughed together then Alex had asked, *"Are you with someone?"*

"Not anymore. You?"

"I've been too busy."'

"So, if I asked you back to my place, you'd be okay with that?"

"More than okay."

"Good. So happens that we've walked far enough to be just a block from my apartment."

They'd quickened their pace and soon had been in Cody's bedroom. *"I owe you a blow job,"* Cody had said, falling to his knees and unzipping Alex's jeans as he did so. They'd spent the rest of the night naked, and having frantic, pent-up sex.

There had been a time when Alex would have smiled at the memory, but now it was a bittersweet remembrance. His gaze flitted to the dining room wall by the window where a black and white study of Cody hung. They had tried to be more to each other than friends, after that first meeting, but Cody had found it hard to shake off the nightmare of Farmton Manor.

Thanks to his Aunt Katherine and the therapist she'd recommended he see, Alex had, over time, managed to deal with most of the PTSD, the trauma that being incarcerated at Farmton had left him with. He'd never forget, nor would he forgive those who had sent him there, those who had tried to beat out of him his strength of spirit and self-worth, but he'd refused to let the awful experience dominate his life, unlike Cody.

Cody... Sweet, gentle Cody with the golden hair and the bluest of eyes had been ill-equipped to deal with the harshness of life at Farmton. He'd arrived during Alex's last year at the manor and it was as if he regarded Alex to be his sole protector, was ever at his side, but silently, afraid to speak above a whisper, and was soon a target for the worst of the bullies. Alex had tried to shield him the best he could, but a seventeen-year-old undernourished kid had been no match against burly adults with twisted perceptions of how those they oversaw should be treated. It was Cody that Alex had been caught with engaging in deviant behavior as Ernest Holloway, the house counselor had called it, before ordering a flogging for them both.

Alex had turned eighteen that year, and his Aunt Katherine had shown up at Farmton to pick him up, and as she told him later, *"I said to that Holloway dickhead, I'm here to collect my nephew and damn anyone who gets in my way!"* No one had gotten in her way, and Alex's last memory of Farmton was of Cody's tearstained face watching Alex leave.

"And I'm doing it again, dammit," Alex muttered under his breath. He reached for what remained of the wine he and Blake had shared earlier. Sometimes the memories, despite his best efforts, were just too raw to suppress.

If he had one major regret, it was that he hadn't tried harder to stop Cody from leaving. Theirs had never been a grand love affair, but there had been a warm and affectionate connection between them that, at first, had helped Alex cope with Cody's, at times, violent mood swings. Sometimes Alex got the impression that Cody resented him, but for what Alex couldn't determine, and of course, Cody would deny it if Alex asked him outright if he'd done something to upset him.

Alex had come to realize that the conversion therapy tactics employed at Farmton had done irreparable damage to Cody, and that no matter how hard he tried, or how many counseling sessions he attended, he just could not shake the trauma of that time. When Cody announced that he was accepting a job transfer to Boston, his hometown, Alex had thought, at first, that it might be a good idea, and he had to admit to a sense of relief that he wouldn't have to deal with the day-to-day stress of living with Cody. They hadn't been lovers. They'd rented an apartment together but they'd had separate bedrooms, yet often the pall of depression had seemed to pervade the entire apartment when Cody fell into one of his moods.

He hadn't blamed himself when he'd heard of Cody's suicide. He'd blamed himself for not putting up more arguments about why Cody shouldn't go to Boston, but he'd seemed so determined that perhaps the transfer was going to open up a new life for him. Alex had believed him in the end. There was enough blame to go around for the tragedy that was Cody. His parents, who'd sent him away to be 'cured' then thrown him out when he went home and told them he was still gay, that the vile treatment he'd endured at Farmton hadn't changed him, hadn't made him the nice little straight boy they'd wanted for a son.

Alex had phoned them, screaming at them, calling them every slur he could think of until they'd hung up on him. He'd called them again, threatening them with arrest as accessories to Cody's death. He'd known he was losing it, but he had been so angry. Cody was dead and it could have been avoided. All he'd wanted was his parents to love him. All he'd wanted was peace, freedom from the nightmares that haunted him almost every night. Well, at least now he was at peace.

Now, staring at Cody's portrait, it seemed that Alex had caught the very essence of his dead friend. That haunted, faraway look in Cody's eyes could still cause pain, as if a hard fist were clenched around his heart.

Alex sighed then swilled the last of his wine and placed the glass in the sink to wash in the morning. It was late and he should go to bed. He doubted that he would sleep, unless he could turn his mind to more pleasant things, like seeing Blake tomorrow…

* * * *

"Oh, thank the Lord!" Blake was a tad startled by Estelle's greeting when she opened the care center door. "He's been buggin' me all morning, asking when you'd be here."

"I'm sorry," Blake said. "I probably shouldn't be doing this. I don't know if I'm making it any better for him or not."

Estelle nodded. "It's good of you to care, but unless you're going to make an application to foster him, it'll just get his hopes up."

"I know, and I feel bad about that. It's just that I'm single, have a one-bedroom apartment and I spend way too much time at work. It wouldn't really be fair for him to be farmed out to daycare all the time."

"Loads of kids have single parents and are in daycare when parents work. He'd have the joy of seeing you when you pick him up at the end of your day."

Blake sighed. "What about the girls?"

"They'll be all right. I already have a family I've contacted about them. A Mr. and Mrs. Fuller. Good people who'll look after them properly. They are coming in this afternoon to meet the girls."

"That's good. And Joey?"

"The Fullers already have two boys, but I'm sure we'll find him a good home. That is…" She gave him a sly look. "If you don't want to step up."

Blake groaned. "Estelle…" He didn't get any further. A small tornado whirled toward him and threw itself on his legs. "Joey, you scamp." Blake hoisted the little guy into his arms. Joey clamped his arms around Blake's neck and pressed his face to Blake's.

Estelle watched them, a small smile on her lips. Blake rolled his eyes at her then laughed when he tried to put Joey down and the kid wouldn't let go of his neck.

"Why not take him to the park on Sixth?" Estelle said. "He could use some fresh air."

"Is that allowed?" Blake asked.

"It is if I say it is. It'll give you time to think and get to know Joey better."

Blake was afraid of getting to know Joey better. He just might not want to let the kid go into the system.

Was he already in way over his head with the almost parental affection he felt for Joey?

"Okay." He knelt so that he was face-to-face with Joey. "Like to go to the park, maybe get some ice cream?"

Joey's little face brightened, and he smiled and nodded vigorously. Blake stood and took Joey's tiny hand in his. Estelle walked them to the door.

"I'll have some reading material for you to look at when you get back. Don't give him too much ice cream — he's already had lunch."

Blake had a hunch about what kind of 'reading material' she meant. *Yep, I'm most definitely in way over my head.*

Chapter Eight

Blake slipped into the gallery foyer just before six. He could see Alex shaking hands with a group of people and he took the time to just stand there and watch with admiration the handsome man who was once more in his life. He had a good feeling about where he and Alex were headed together. He'd experienced the gradual slipping away of his usual wariness when it came to the 'getting to know you' stage of a new relationship.

Not that he and Alex were new by any means. As boys, they'd been inseparable. As teenagers they'd been lovers, and now, it seemed that in their thirties, they might just be lovers again. He hoped so, anyway. Early days, without a doubt, but somehow it felt *right*.

Of course, he'd yet to tell Alex about Joey and what effect the little boy might have on Blake's life if he decided to go through with applying to be Joey's foster father. Estelle had pressed a package of papers into his hand before he'd left the care center. He hadn't opened the package, but he knew what was in it. He stepped back when the doors to the gallery opened and several people passed by, raving about the exhibition. Alex and Doreen were the stragglers, their heads together in deep conversation. Alex smiled at Blake as he and Doreen drew near.

"Don't think you've met officially?" Alex tugged Doreen forward to meet Blake.

"Of course we have," Doreen said, smiling at Blake. "If it hadn't been for me, I don't think you'd be trying to introduce us, Alex."

"You're right," Blake said. "You more or less pushed me inside here, for which I'm very grateful. Good to meet you again."

"Charming *and* good-looking." Doreen patted Alex's arm. "I think you have a keeper here, Alex."

"That's what I envy you for, Doreen," Alex said, coloring slightly. "Your degree in subtlety…not."

Blake grinned, although his cheeks were hot too. Doreen tittered. "Well, I won't keep you from your date. See you next week, Alex, and I hope to see *you* again soon, Blake." With that she sauntered away toward the door with the frosted glass and gold lettering.

"Sorry about that," Alex muttered. "She loves playing matchmaker. Anyway…" He took Blake's arm and led him outside. "How's your day been?"

"Pretty good." He didn't think the time to tell Alex about the day's events was while they were walking down Broadway. "Where are we going?"

"Well, I'm famished, otherwise I'd take you somewhere, like my apartment where I could taste those lush lips of yours again. But there's no food there, so I was thinking about a new restaurant that's getting rave reviews, and it's just a short walk to the corner."

"Sounds good. Did you have a productive afternoon?"

"Yeah. Doreen's extending the exhibition for another two weeks."

Blake frowned. "Where will you go when it ends?"

"Probably on tour. I'll keep the apartment here though. I like LA…even more now I know you're here."

"When you say 'tour', what does that mean in terms of weeks or months?"

"Not *months*. A month maybe, or a couple of weeks here and there."

"Oh." Blake sighed with relief. He'd just had a sick feeling in the pit of his stomach thinking about Alex gone for months on end.

"You'd miss me already?" Alex teased.

"Yes," Blake replied. "I've just got you back."

Alex slowed his steps then turned to face Blake, a sensual smile on his lips. "You know, I've gotten over being famished. What d'you say we Uber back to my place and pick up where we left off last night?"

"I think that's a helluvan idea."

* * * *

Alex could tell there was no doubt in Blake's mind what Alex had meant by picking up where they'd left off last night. They were barely through the door when Blake pulled him into his arms and delivered a kiss that sent thrills through every fiber of Alex's body and made him weak at the knees. Blake's lips were soft and warm, tender, but with a demanding edge that made Alex want more and he returned the kiss willingly, eagerly, gliding his tongue over Blake's as he opened to him.

My God, this man can kiss. Slow mover, my ass!

Pressed up against the wall by the door, Alex gave in to Blake's passion, wrapping his arms around Blake's slim waist and pushing his groin into Blake's, frotting on the hard bulge that matched his own. The desire for more was overwhelming. He wanted Blake naked, wanted to feel that hard, lean body slide over his, wanted to taste, inhale every part of him.

The kiss they shared deepened, their tongues tussled and their mouths ground together. They swallowed each other's breath, inhaling each other's taste and scent, the erotic sensations running through Alex's body bringing him too close to the brink of release.

"Wait, wait," he gasped, pulling away slightly. "It's been a while for me. I'm gonna come in my pants if we keep this up."

"Can't have that," Blake said, unbuckling Alex's belt then pulling his zipper down. He freed Alex's erection from his briefs, his hand warm and firm around the hard flesh. "Feels so damned good, Alex," he murmured before falling to his knees, taking Alex's pants and briefs with him. He nuzzled Alex's balls. "Smells good too." He gripped Alex's cock at its base then licked and kissed his way up the hard pulsing length.

Alex groaned at the touch of Blake's tongue as he swept it over the head, licking at the salty pre-cum that bubbled up from the slit. Alex ran his fingers through Blake's dark curly hair and gave himself up to the thrill of Blake's warm, wet mouth enclosing his throbbing shaft. He knew he couldn't last and he got ready to warn Blake of his impending climax.

"*Blake.*" It was little more than a croak, and Blake either didn't hear him or was ignoring his warning. Blake ran his hands up and down Alex's thighs then palmed Alex's ass cheeks and pulled him further into his mouth, his throat muscles clenching around Alex's cockhead.

Oh my God, no one has made me feel like this. So many emotions and sensations all at the same time. I want to come and yet I don't want to 'cause then it'll be over, and what he's doing to me should be fucking illegal. Oh my God, I can't hold back. "Blake! Oh my God!" he roared.

He was weak at the knees again and only Blake's arms around him stopped him from sinking to the floor. He'd never come so hard and fast in his life. His entire body convulsed in the throes of post-orgasmic ecstasy.

"Blake," he whispered when he was finally released from Blake's lips and he could kneel in front of him and kiss him and hold him as if he'd never let him go. He could taste himself on Blake's tongue, and his head swam from the sensation. No man had ever gone this far with him before. Not even Cody, who didn't like to swallow, nor the two other men who'd given him blow jobs in the back room of the first gay bar he'd visited in LA. Blake and he had tasted each other when they'd been boys, unsure at first then with more gusto when they'd discovered they liked it — a lot.

Alex chuckled at the memory, and Blake tapped him on the nose with his forefinger and raised an eyebrow. "What's so funny?"

"I was remembering the first time we tasted each other's cum. That was a moment I could never forget."

"Right, and you taste sweet, just like you did then."

"Thank you. And I can't wait to return the favor."

"Maybe we should get off the floor." Blake grinned. "My knees are cramping."

"How about the bed?" Alex stood, offered Blake his hand then heaved him to his feet. They kissed briefly before Alex kicked off his shoes. "No point in keeping my pants on either," he said, laughing.

"Right. I'd just haul them off you anyway."

"Mmm, sounds like fun." Alex pulled up his zipper. "Get ready to haul away."

Arms around each other, they hurried into the bedroom. They were naked and on top of the bed in less than a minute, the only holdup being when Alex insisted on making it difficult for Blake to haul his pants off as threatened.

They were laughing like idiots by the time Blake held them up in triumph. It was like they were young boys again, horsing around like they'd done in the swimming hole or in the woods where they'd found their secret place. And, just as then, their laughter quickly morphed into moans and sighs of pleasure. Blake climbed on top of Alex and laid claim to his lips with a deep and sensuous kiss that thrilled Alex all the way down to his toes, which curled in blissful response.

To Blake, Alex's familiar face and body, sculpted from scrawny boyhood to toned and lean muscled manhood, was like coming home. There had been only a few men in his life, and not for very long. And now that Alex was back in his arms, he knew the reason why. No one had compared with Alex. Even after all the years apart this seemed so right. No other man had made him feel wanted, the way Alex did now. The way he returned Blake's kisses like he couldn't get enough of them, his soft, warm lips parting under Blake's, his tongue gliding, twisting inside Blake's mouth, searching out the most sensitive parts, making Blake see stars, and harder than a rock.

Earlier, Alex had said he was unforgettable. He'd been joking, but Blake knew it to be true. Alex was unforgettable in every way, and when he thought about it, and he had ever since their reunion, despite the years that had separated them, he'd never forgotten Alex.

This is heaven. No, scratch that. It's better than heaven. Alex's naked body pressed to his, the warm smooth skin covering the hot body that writhed under him, a sensation like no other he'd ever experienced. He wanted to kiss every part of Alex, loath as he was to pull away from Alex's lips.

He nuzzled Alex's throat, sucked lightly on his Adam's apple and kissed his shoulders, his chest, lingering over each tiny nipple, licking, nibbling until they responded by hardening under his tongue. He dragged his mouth down over Alex's hard torso, stopping only when he reached the curly pubes that crowned Alex's pulsing erection. Blake inhaled the musky scent of spent cum from Alex's previous orgasm, an aphrodisiac to his senses.

Blake gripped Alex's cock at the base then took it between his lips, licking over the glistening slit, savoring the slick pre-cum that pooled on his tongue. Alex cried out when Blake devoured him with one long swallow of the entire length, with just a hint of teeth around the base, scraping gently over the tender skin. Alex bucked his hips, and Blake welcomed the sudden thrust into his mouth with a hard suck. He gripped Alex's cock at the hilt and pulled back.

"That's it, babe," he murmured. "Fuck my mouth, give me all of it." *So much for my reputation of taking it slow. But Alex is just so incredible. Gorgeous and incredible.*

Alex pumped upward again, and Blake took it all, at the same time cupping Alex's balls, caressing them tenderly with his fingers. Alex moaned and ran his hands over and through Blake's curls, tugging them each time he jerked his hips upward and drove his cock into Blake's mouth.

"Mmm…" Blake hummed with satisfaction while he sucked, swirling his tongue around the hard length. Releasing Alex's balls, he slid two fingers over his taint and teased his hole, probing gently before pushing his middle finger into Alex's hot core. Alex writhed over Blake's finger, drawing him in farther, and Blake savored the spurts of pre-cum on his tongue as he massaged Alex's prostate.

"I want to come with you inside me," Alex whispered. "And I'm really, really close again."

Blake withdrew his finger and knelt between Alex's thighs. He leaned in to kiss him on the lips. "Okay. You have lube and a condom?"

Alex nodded. "Nightstand drawer. I stopped by the pharmacy on the way home yesterday, just in case."

Blake smiled. "Had me figured out, huh?"

"Not really. I was just hopeful we'd get to use them at some point."

"To be honest I didn't think we'd get this far, this fast," Blake said. "I told you I was a slow mover, and now it looks like I'm a no-good liar."

Alex smiled and reached up to caress Blake's face. "A beautiful liar."

Blake opened the drawer. "Whoa, that's quite the supply."

"Told you I was hopeful."

Alex pulled Blake down to claim his lips again. He just couldn't get enough of Blake's kisses. The feel, the taste, the scent of him made Alex slightly manic with desire. There was no doubt in his mind that he loved Blake, was falling in love with him, all over again. *Screw the years in between.* They were together again, just as it always had meant to be.

"Blake," he breathed into Blake's mouth. "Fuck me, please. I can't wait to have you inside me." It amazed him how much he wanted this. He'd never craved it like he did now. Before, it was something he'd endured to make the other guy happy. But with Blake he knew it would be something really special.

After another hard kiss, Blake knelt between Alex's thighs and sheathed himself while Alex watched, licking his lips in expectation of Blake's beautiful hard cock driving its way into him. Alex raised his hips and legs to give Blake access for his lube-slicked fingers. He shuddered when Blake penetrated him with one then two fingers, easing his way into Alex's eager hole, curling around that special place that gave a man sensations like no other.

"Oh yeah..." Alex's eyes rolled back, and he gave himself up to the delicious pleasure Blake was bringing him. Blake leaned in to suck on Alex's nipples, causing Alex to gasp and writhe under him. "Feels so good, Blako." He wriggled his ass over Blake's fingers, taking more of him. "Now your cock." He smiled up at Blake. "I know, bossy."

Blake chuckled. "Your wish, O master."

Alex grabbed at Blake's shoulders and arched into him as he pushed forward, breaching Alex's tight resistance. "Uh…" Yeah, it burned some. Alex had expected it. Like he'd said earlier, it had been a while, but he wanted this, really wanted it, and he knew the pain would diminish and become pleasure, the deeper Blake went.

"Breathe, Alex," Blake whispered, his lips on Alex's mouth.

Alex held him there, opening to him and the all-consuming kiss they shared took away the pain. He blew out a deep sigh of satisfaction when Blake slid all the way inside him with one long, sure stroke. He wound his legs around Blake's waist and held on tight while Blake began to thrust with a slow and sensuous rhythm.

Alex thought maybe he was having an out-of-body experience. It had never felt like this before. Blake buried inside him was the best thing that had happened to him in the last twenty years.

"Okay?" Blake asked, panting slightly, sweat glistening on his forehead. Alex knew he had never seen anyone as beautiful as the man who now owned him body and soul. *But he always has, hasn't he?* There were no words he could form at that moment. His only reply was the low keening sound of pleasure coming from deep in his throat. That seemed to inflame Blake and he quickened the pace of his thrusts, filling Alex with his steel-hard cock. He rammed into him, pistoning his hips with a fierceness that had Alex holding him even tighter and moaning almost loud enough to alert the neighborhood *watch.*

Blake muffled him with his lips and tongue, their kiss adding to the urgency that swept through Alex's body, setting every nerve ending in him afire. He gripped his erection and came violently, falling apart after only two strokes of his hand. His body convulsed, and a stream of white-hot cum sprayed across his chest and up under Blake's chin.

He rocked and shuddered in Blake's arms, telling him in whispered tones how incredible he was and that he was the best. *The* best. Blake moved hard and fast inside Alex, clearly desperate now to find his own release. Alex clung to him as his body stiffened and he came, a stifled growl escaping him before he took Alex's lips again with a searing kiss that was close to melting Alex's brain.

He lay over Alex, his face nestled in the hollow between Alex's neck and shoulder, tracing tender kisses over the warm skin. Alex held him, amazed and slightly shaken by the intensity of their mating. He wanted to hold Blake like this all through the night, drift off to sleep in each other's arms, awaken to start a new day with the promise of endless days together.

Well, I can dream, can't I?

Chapter Nine

Blake woke with a start, then on realizing where he was, settled into the warmth of the body pressed to his. Alex had asked Blake to stay the night after the third time they'd had sex. Blake had accepted the offer, because he really didn't want to leave the solid comfort of Alex's body or the coziness of his bed. Three times was a definite record for him. Bradford had never wanted to even attempt a second round, regardless of how much Blake had tried to coax him. Sex with Alex had taken him to a whole new plane of existence. The man was a wonder. He brushed his hand over Alex's soft sandy-blond hair and smiled when Alex snuggled even closer, his arm wrapped around Blake's chest.

Tomorrow was Sunday, so they'd planned to spend the day together. Blake wondered if Alex would like the idea of visiting the care center and meeting Joey. He hadn't told him much about his thoughts for Joey's well-being, and was right now the best time to bring up the possibility of him fostering the little boy? He wasn't sure himself if he could go through with it. It was such an enormous responsibility. He would have to rearrange his entire schedule, and would his bosses even go for it?

The time in the park he'd shared with Joey had been a delight. Considering what he'd been through in his few years of life, he'd been remarkably attentive and well-behaved, not like some of the screaming kids playing nearby.

Joey had never left his side, holding on to his hand while they'd walked and cuddling into him when they'd sat on a park bench. The only time Blake hadn't had his full attention was when a golden retriever had wandered over and put its head on Blake's knee. After a quick glance, Blake had ascertained the dog was male and he'd gazed at both Blake and Joey from soulful eyes. Blake hadn't been able to resist stroking his head and tickling him under the chin. Joey had slipped off the bench and wrapped his arms around the retriever's neck, and for a moment Blake had almost seen his future.

Alex, Joey, a golden retriever and him, all together as a family.

Oh boy. You really are delusional. Alex might be a tad surprised that one make-out session and a sex-filled sleepover would result in him fostering a little boy and getting a family dog. And a house. They'd have to have a house to make this all complete. He suppressed his laughter for fear of waking Alex, then yawned so wide his jaw cracked.

I guess I'll think about it tomorrow…

* * * *

The next day, after they'd taken full advantage of each other's early morning wood then showered together, they walked to the neighborhood diner that had become Alex's favorite since he'd moved to Pasadena. "I think you'll like it," he said, twining his fingers through Blake's as they walked down one of Pasadena's many tree-lined streets. A warm breeze rustled the leaves above them while the sun laid dappled shadows on the sidewalk. They glanced at each other and smiled.

"I'm sure I will," Blake murmured, squeezing Alex's hand. "So far, I've liked everything we've done together. I see you brought your camera."

"Thought I'd get a few casual shots of you, if you're okay with that."

"Long as you get my good side."

They stepped out of the way to let two women pushing a baby carriage pass. The women smiled their thanks, and Alex peeked at the baby.

"Cute kid."

"You like kids?" Blake thought it might be a good idea to know, just in case.

"Yeah." He bumped Blake's shoulder. "Can't have any though. Wrong plumbing."

Blake chuckled. "Idiot."

"And on the fourth day, he declared I was an idiot," Alex intoned. "Didn't take long to figure it out."

"You're not an idiot. I don't date idiots."

"Oh, we're dating?" Alex stared at him with mock alarm and pressed a hand to his chest. "Be still my heart."

Blake laughed. "Stop that." Then he frowned. "We are, aren't we?"

"Well, I'm dating you, Blako," Alex said, grinning.

"Oh, that's all right then."

Alex slipped an arm around Blake's waist and pulled him close. They'd reached the diner, and he pushed the door open so he could usher Blake in with a courtly bow and a pat on his ass. "Mmm," he murmured. "Feels great, just like it did last night, and this morning."

"Behave," Blake muttered, but flashed Alex a grin.

The diner was busy with a lively crowd. The hostess showed them to a table in the corner by the window and Alex waved to a couple of people they passed on their way through the other tables.

"You come here often?" Blake teased.

"I used to come every Sunday until I got so busy with the gallery and doing out-of-town stuff." He unslung his camera from his shoulder as he sat facing Blake. "Has anyone ever told you you're a handsome devil?"

Blake's cheeks pinked. "Not in those exact words, until you."

"Well, you are. The classic look with that square chin and chiseled cheekbones, but with an underlying devilish quality, that for me, is a gigantic turn-on."

"*Alex...*" Blake was blushing like mad now. "You have no idea what you're doing to me right now."

Alex winked. "Oh, yes I do." He shut up when a young woman wearing a dark green uniform appeared at their table.

"Hi, I'm Cindi. What can I get you boys to drink?"

"Coffee, please, and an orange juice."

"Safome," Blake croaked. "I mean, same for me, sorry." He shot Alex an evil look when she turned away to get their order.

"You're adorable," Alex said.

"And you're a brat. Tell me why I'm sitting here with you again?"

"Because you think I'm adorable too?"

Blake huffed. "I suppose that's it."

Alex cackled. "No supposing about it!" He clamped his lips together when Cindi showed up carrying their coffees and juices.

"Decide on anything to eat?"

"Uh, yeah, I'll have the Denver omelet," Alex told her with a winning smile.

"The same, please," Blake muttered. He hadn't even glanced at the menu, but a Denver sounded good.

"You guys are easy to please." Cindi said cheerfully. "Be right back."

"Good to know." Alex winked at him.

"What is?"

"That you're easy to please."

Blake frowned. "Don't even."

"What d'you mean?"

"You were going to drop that old cliché about me being easy to please 'cause I'm with you."

"Was not."

"Was too!" Blake started to laugh. "My God, what are we, five?"

Alex joined in. "Less than that, methinks. Anyway..." He reached for Blake's hand and held it gently. "Just so you know, I aim to please you in every way I can, in and out of the bed."

"That's sweet." Blake ran his thumb over Alex's fingers. "And just so you know, you've already pleased me, in every possible way."

"See, I knew it. You really are easy to please!"

"Cut that out!" Their laughter caused other diners to turn and stare at them. Blake ducked his head. "Now look what you've done."

"Glad you boys are having such a good time," Cindi said, laying their omelets in front of them. "Can I get you anything else?"

"A different dining partner?" Blake suggested, smirking.

"Oh, you know you love me," Alex countered. "Doesn't he, Cindi?"

"I'm sure he does," Cindi murmured. "So eat up, boys. Gotta keep your strength up."

"What did she mean by that?" Blake whispered.

Alex waggled his eyebrows. "Exactly what you thought she meant."

"Oh, my God. We can never come here again."

* * * *

After breakfast, they strolled through the park at the end of the street. For a Sunday, it was remarkably quiet. As far as Blake could see, they were the only ones on the footpath and there were no sounds of children playing nearby, nor adult voices raised in conversation.

"So I was wondering," Blake said. "How would you feel about coming with me to see Joey at the care center? I kinda promised him I'd stop by this afternoon." Sensing a moment's hesitation from Alex, Blake added, "It's okay if you'd rather not. I can go by myself, and we could hook up again later today."

"No, it's good. I'll come with you. I don't really want you out of my sight for the rest of the day." He put an arm around Blake's shoulders, and warbled off-key,

"Stuck like glue, you and me, baby, we're stuck like glue."

Blake laughed. "Don't give up your day job just yet."

"Ouch. I'll have you know I was much in demand in the Bakerton Elementary school choir."

"You were not. We were both in that choir, and neither one of us was 'much in demand'."

"True that. I can still see old, uh, what was his name?"

"Mr. Bryant."

"Yeah, him, scrunching up his face when we were caterwauling at the tops of our voices."

"I think that was more you than me," Blake said, grinning. "I knew I couldn't sing so I kept it down. You made me laugh so hard when you went for those high notes."

"Yeah, the good old days when everything was just you and me." He tightened his hold on Blake's shoulder and drew him in closer to his side. "You ever think about what might have happened, to *us* I mean, if my parents hadn't sent me away?"

"Yes. After we met in the gallery, and I remembered how close we'd been when we were boys, I couldn't help but wonder if we would've stayed connected, gone on through life together. I know it would have been what I wanted. Back then I couldn't imagine anyone taking your place. You were my best friend, and I loved you."

"So turning the past into the present," Alex said, close to Blake's ear. "You are still my best friend, and I still love you." He steered Blake toward a bench under the trees. "And right now, I want to capture that kinda stunned expression on your face."

"I'm not stunned. Just wary I guess. It's only been four days."

Alex slipped his camera off his shoulder. "Twenty years and four days, and that is long enough to know you love someone. That someone being you."

Blake sat on the bench looking up at Alex. He couldn't help but smile at Alex's matter-of-factness.

"That's better. You're even more beautiful when you smile." Alex pulled his camera from its bag and, after fiddling with it for a few moments, crouched down and focused it on Blake. "Okay, look straight at me and lose that smile."

"I thought you'd want me to say cheese."

"I want you to say a lot of things, but cheese isn't one of them. Now, turn your head just a bit then look at me."

"I thought you said to look straight at you."

"I got that one. Just do what I say, please."

"Wow, bossy." Blake turned as instructed but couldn't help smirking at Alex's tone. *In and out of bed.*

"Oh, that's good. That's so good. The upturned corner of your mouth. I love it. Now look up into the branches over your head. Not too much, a bit lower, please. Good, now, can you loosen your shirt collar, or better still take your shirt off."

"Really?"

"Yes, really."

"What if someone comes by?"

"Blake, it's your shirt, not your entire ensemble. We saw guys shirtless lying on the grass on the way here."

"Okay." Blake pulled his shirt over his head and laid it on the bench. "Now what?"

"Sit back, spread your arms along the back of the bench, and look pensive."

Blake laughed. "Pensive?"

"Yes, like you're thinking about something earth-shattering, like sex."

"Okay, I'll just look at you and remember last night and this morning."

"If you're trying to make me hard, you're on the right track. Okay, raise one leg and drape an arm over it, sit upright, tilt your head to the left, now the right. God, you're sexy."

Blake figured Alex must have taken a hundred photos of him. His neck was starting to ache. "Can you take one of us together, like a selfie?" Blake asked in between poses.

"Please. With *this* camera? Sacrilege."

Blake rolled his eyes. "Okay, we can use my phone."

"Fine, but I want some more headshots of you first."

"I feel like a model."

"Believe me, you're a whole lot better looking than some of the models I've worked with."

"Oh, you do that too?"

"Yep. Bread and butter. Gives me the freedom to do the stuff I really love. Okay…" He put his camera away and came to sit with Blake on the bench. He pulled his phone out of his pocket. "Okay, lover, snuggle up and say *cheeeese*."

* * * *

They took Blake's car downtown to the care center. "Not the best part of town," Alex remarked when he got out of the car and looked around at the dingy street.

"No, it's not, but the budget doesn't stretch for a better location," Blake told him. "It's clean inside and comfortable enough, and there's a park with a playground on the corner where I took him yesterday."

Estelle opened the door and beamed at Blake. "I saw you pull up," she said. "Joey's been excited since I told him you might stop by to see him."

"How is he?" Blake asked. "More settled?"

"Yes and no. He has his moments." Her gaze flicked to Alex.

"Estelle, this is my friend, Alex. We were schoolmates back in the day."

Alex extended his hand. "Pleased to meet you, Estelle."

"Oh, lordy, this is my lucky day." Estelle looked as if she wouldn't let go of Alex any time soon. "Two fine-looking men at the same time. You both'd be the answer to any girl's prayer." Her dark cheeks flushed, and she rolled her eyes at herself. "Oh, listen to me goin' on. Here's Joey to save me from making a fool of myself."

"Brake!" Joey ran at Blake in his usual high-spirited fashion, and Blake caught him up in his arms and swung him around, Joey's peals of laughter filling the hallway. Before he got too dizzy, Blake put him down and turned him to face Alex.

"Joey, this is my best friend, Alex. We've known each other since we were your age — well almost your age. Maybe since we were five."

Joey gazed up at Alex who smiled and held out his hand. Joey fastened his little fingers onto Alex's. "Sing me too," he commanded in his piping voice, and Alex, of course, obeyed, swinging him high over his head until Estelle clapped her hands over her ears to deaden Joey's happy shrieking.

"Oh, my Lord, put him down before I lose both my eardrums!"

"Is it okay if we take him to the park?" Blake asked after Alex set Joey on his feet. Joey didn't leave their side, but stared up at Blake and Alex as if deciding which man he liked better. Blake didn't miss the little guy's calculating gaze.

"You can take him for an hour," Estelle told them, "but don't go giving him any treats or he won't eat his dinner."

"How are Loren and Emily?"

"Just fine. Keren's taken them over to see Mr. and Mrs. Fuller. They had a nice meeting yesterday afternoon and this'll be a kind of follow-up to see if the girls are bonding with them. I think it'll go well—the Fullers are a lot nicer people than the Harrises."

"They couldn't be any nastier, that's for sure," Blake said, ruffling Joey's hair. "Wanna go on the swings again, Joey?"

"Yay!" Joey jumped up and down then grabbed Blake's hand, trying to pull him toward the door. Blake traded looks with Estelle, and he could tell what she was thinking. But was he ready to take on the responsibility that fostering would bring him—and where would that put his and Alex's future together? *If there is to be such a thing.*

Was it too soon to be thinking like this? Alex had said he loved him, and he knew his feelings for Alex went way beyond just besties, but they'd only been reunited a few days. There were so many things to consider here and throwing Joey into the mix might just be a recipe for disaster. Yet, seeing Joey holding on to Alex's hand as he skipped along happily between them, it just felt so right.

"What d'you like best in the playpark, Joey?" Alex asked.

"Sings!" Joey declared.

"Okay, swings, I like them too. You can push me on one if you like."

Joey looked at him doubtfully. "You're too *big*."

"Blako will help."

"Who Brako?"

"Oh my God," Blake said through his laughter. "You gonna start calling me *Brako*, now, Alex?"

"That's not a bad idea. I like it, Brako."

"No you don't. Joey doesn't like it either. Do you, Joey?"

Joey nodded. "Like it."

"Drat."

"Can't wait to whisper it in your ear later when we uh, you know."

"That might just be a deal breaker."

Alex snorted. "No chance."

They'd reached the park and Joey ran on ahead with an excited shout of "Sings!"

"He really is a great kid," Alex said. "You said his foster parents abused him. How could anyone beat on a cute kid like that?"

"Estelle wants me to fill out an application to foster Joey," Blake said quickly and waited for Alex's reaction.

"Oh, yeah?" Alex gazed at Blake. "Is that what you want to do?"

"I want Joey to have foster parents who will love him and give him a good life." Blake sighed. "I don't know if I have what it takes to fill that role. I mean I spend the whole day either in the office or at the courthouse. I only have a one-bedroom apartment with a tiny den. He'd have to attend preschool. I just don't know if I can be enough for him."

"But you'd give him what he needs most of all...a kind and loving father." Alex ran a hand over Blake's arm. "Loads of kids have single parents and some go to daycare because both parents work. That's something you could work out, and I'd be glad to help."

They were distracted by Joey's impatient voice yelling, "Push, Brako!"

Alex laughed. "Go, Brako. Do your fatherly duty."

Blake groaned. It would seem as if the decision were being made for him. Alex grinned and got his camera ready.

Chapter Ten

"Are you hungry?" Blake asked as he pulled away from the care center.

"Kind of. That ice cream didn't do much for me. Joey liked it though."

"Yeah, let's hope he doesn't tell Estelle about it."

Alex suggested they stop for take out on the way back to his place. "Or did you want to go home?"

"If you come with me."

"Okay. I haven't seen your place yet."

"It's nothing much." He smiled. "Doesn't have any Alexander Martin artwork on the walls."

Alex ran a hand over Blake's thigh and squeezed gently. "We'll have to remedy that."

"Something else you'll have to remedy if you keep that up," Blake said, his voice sounding thick.

"It'll be my pleasure." He leaned over the console so he could kiss Blake on the cheek. "That's a little down payment on the much larger sum you'll get later."

Blake turned his face so he could reach Alex's mouth and they enjoyed a brief but sensuous lip-lock.

"So, about Joey," Alex said, sliding back into his seat. "I saw Estelle corner you before we left."

"Yeah, she said she needs my application in ASAP, or he'll go into the system and the next family in line will be interviewed for placement." Blake sighed. "I don't want him to end up in an endless cycle of foster homes until he's eighteen, like so many of these kids do."

"But you're not fully committed."

"Only because of what I've said before. Long hours at work, and my apartment is small. Those two things are enough to go against my application. Joey needs stability and a good family to grow up in."

"Or a loving dad who'll juggle his career enough to make sure Joey is looked after by skilled people during the day and who will enlist the help of friends, mainly me, to fill in when they can. I said I'll help, Blako. You know you want to do this, so at least make the attempt."

"But if it all goes to hell, the kid will be upset. He's already going to be anxious when the girls go to their new foster home."

"Is that a done deal?"

"Looks like. Estelle said the second meeting went well, so it could be wrapped up in a few days."

"Oh, stop at the next light. There's a real good Italian restaurant that does a takeout lasagna. Fancy that?"

"Sounds good."

"Okay. I'll leap out and you can circle the block. There's nowhere to park so this is the best way to get what we want."

"Okay." Blake pulled over to let Alex out then cruised to the next corner and made the turn. So, Alex was on board with him fostering Joey or, at least, making the application. It would be so much easier if he and Alex were married, but it was crazy to even mention that after the few days they'd been reunited. In his heart he knew Alex was the one for him, always had been, but even so, they had to take the time to get to know each other as adult men.

Alex was a gorgeous man, perfect really, and yes, they were truly compatible in bed, and they enjoyed each other's company, but was that enough? Wasn't it all too soon? And if his application to foster Joey went through but something happened to break Alex and him up, what then? There were just too many damned variables.

He had to circle the block twice before he spotted Alex standing on the corner clutching a large brown bag to his chest. "You get the monster size?" he teased as Alex climbed into the car.

"No, but I did get us a salad, a baguette and a bottle of red wine. So we're all set for culinary delights this evening."

"We have to split the cost."

"No, we don't. This is my treat."

"But you got the pizza the other night. If this is going to be a relationship that works, it has to be fifty-fifty."

"Who sez?" Alex poked him in the ribs.

"I sez, and ouch! Want me to rear-end that car in front?"

"No, I want you to rear-end me before dinner."

"You sure have a strange way of trying to romance a guy."

"I have a lot of strange ways." He walked his fingers up and down Blake's thigh. "Which you will discover as time goes by."

"That didn't sound at all sinister. And cut that out. You're making me hard."

"Good, keep it that way for the rear-ending bit."

Blake couldn't help but love Alex even more after that.

Once inside Blake's apartment, he grabbed the bag from Alex, turned on the oven and shoved the lasagnas inside. He held up the wine bottle. "Wine with sex?"

"Nah, it'd just get in the way. The only thing long and hard I want is between your legs." He ignored Blake's shocked snort and had a quick look around. "This is nice, Blake." His gaze fell on the coffee table where two books on photography lay. "Wow, Arnold Gitmer. You're a fan?"

"Didn't even know who he was till the other day." Blake tried not to look embarrassed but from the sly smile on Alex's face he figured he'd failed. "I stopped in at a downtown bookstore and looked around for this kind of book. I wanted to know more about what you do and maybe what had inspired you."

"That's sweet, Blako."

"But here's the bonus." He picked up the other book. "Alexander Martin. You didn't tell me there was a book with your work in it. And not only that, a bio and pictures of you." He flicked over the pages until he found the one he wanted. "You, without a shirt on and skimpy shorts in the great outdoors. You look amazing."

Alex stared at the photograph. "It was in *Vanity Fair*. They were running a feature on up-and-coming American artists and they included me."

"Wish I read *Vanity Fair*. I'd have been thinking, hey, I know this guy while I was ogling your pecs and the bulge in your shorts."

Alex leaned in to kiss Blake. "You are adorable."

"As are you, sir." They set the books back down on the table so they could hold each other and kiss properly.

"What's the bedroom like?" Alex whispered.

"C'mon, Mr. Subtle." Blake took Alex's hand. "I don't want to keep you in suspense too long." He pushed the bedroom door open and ushered Alex inside, cupping his ass cheeks as he guided him across the room.

"Now what?" Alex gave him a cheeky smile.

Blake threw him down on the bed and climbed on top of him. "You know what. What you've been craving all day. You and me having sex. Me inside you, fucking the cum outta you."

Alex's eyes blazed with desire. "Okay, you're never going to convince me that you're a slow mover, ever again."

"Your fault. You're just so damned amazing. I get hard just thinking about you." He tugged at the hem of Alex's polo and pulled it up and over his head. "Look at you," he whispered. "That beautiful chest. A sculptor's dream." He lowered his head to feast on Alex's tiny nipples.

Alex writhed under him and ran his hands through Blake's curls holding him gently in place while Blake licked and nibbled his way from one pebbled bud to the next.

"Get naked," Alex said.

"Yes, sir." Blake grinned at him and shucked off his T-shirt. Alex's admiring gaze flitted over Blake's defined torso. "Like what you see?"

"More than like." He ran his hands over the dusting of dark curly hair on Blake's chest before fumbling with

Blake's belt. "Want to see all of you." Blake raised himself so that Alex could pull his shorts down along with his briefs. "There it is," Alex murmured. "Long and hard and beautiful." He cupped Blake's ass cheeks, holding him in position as he teased Blake's cockhead with his tongue, lapping at the pre-cum that spilled from the slit.

Blake shuddered from the visceral sensation and from the view of Alex's mouth enveloping his erection, lush lips gliding up and down the rigid length. He wasn't going to compare what Alex was doing with his ex or any of the other few men he'd been with, because there was no comparison. A blow job had never given him this impossible high before. Once again Alex was proving to be the most incredible lover he'd ever had. *And please, God, let no one take him from me!*

He framed Alex's face with his hands, forcing him to look up. *Want him to see the ecstasy on my face, want him to know he's the best.* His loud groan of pleasure made Alex's eyes sparkle, and he sucked harder then pushed Blake onto his back, taking his shorts and briefs completely off him, all the while never releasing Blake from his mouth.

Blake widened his legs and combed his fingers through Alex's soft sandy-blond hair. Alex cupped Blake's balls and ran his tongue over the sac then under it, along his taint to his hole. Blake knew he was going to explode any second. He gritted his teeth and exerted all his willpower to not come in Alex's mouth, but the guy wasn't making it easy.

"Need to taste you too," he said with a note of desperation.

Alex released him and looked up, mischief in his expression. He swung his body around so that his dick was a tantalizing inch or so from Blake's mouth, then resumed his sucking.

Blake didn't hesitate. He gripped Alex's erection at its base then ran his tongue up the hot length before devouring the head, taking it all the way to the back of his throat. He heard Alex gasp. It sounded as if Alex was loving this too, which was what he wanted, although the rock-hard shaft pulsing in his mouth was a pretty sure proof of Alex's enjoyment.

Blake slid his lips up and down over the rigid, throbbing length, relishing every glorious inch of it while he caressed and teased Alex's balls, bringing muffled groans of pleasure from him. Blake stroked Alex's butt, squeezing the twin globes of smooth round flesh, dipping into the cleft and probing at Alex's opening. Alex moaned when Blake slid a finger inside him. His cock pulsed and spilled pre-cum on Blake's tongue and Blake pushed his finger farther inside Alex, finding his sweet spot, causing him to suck harder and cup Blake's ass so he could pull him deeper into his mouth.

Blake was so close, and he knew from the way Alex's body had stiffened then spasmed against him that he was right there with him. Blake almost choked on the torrent of hot, salty cream that filled his mouth, but he tightened his arms around Alex's waist, swallowing him, holding him as he groaned out his pleasure and his body convulsed.

He teetered on the edge of orgasm then yelled when his release overwhelmed him and he came with great body-wracking jolts.

Recovering from that euphoric high wasn't easy, especially as Blake wanted to hang on to the bliss enveloping him. Had sex always been this terrific? *Yes.*

Or rather, it had been since he and Alex had found each other again. But before, not so much. There was no point in comparing what he had now with before. It just didn't exist.

They both lay quietly for a few moments, letting their breathing return to normal. Blake was content to stay, his face buried in Alex's groin, inhaling the scent of spent cum and musk. At Alex's insistence, he scooted back to his original position, tightened his arms around Alex and nuzzled his throat, licking his Adam's apple then sucking lightly on it. He laid his head on Alex's chest, listening to the steady beat of his heart while Alex combed his fingers through Blake's hair.

"What are you thinking?" he asked.

"That I've never been happier," Alex replied. "That I hope this isn't all a dream, and you'll not vanish in a puff of smoke as if the last few days had never happened."

"Not going to vanish." Blake kissed Alex's chest. "I think you should start resigning yourself to the fact that we're back in each other's lives for good. I hope that doesn't alarm you too much."

Alex continued to caress Blake's hair. "Don't hear any alarm bells going off. But I do have an empty void in my belly. It's wondering where all that delicious Italian food went."

Blake grinned, pecked Alex's nose and slid off the bed. "C'mon then…a quick shower then we'll eat."

"Good idea, then we'll be strong enough for round two."

"Or even three."

"How about four?"

"Let's not push our luck." Blake threw an arm around Alex's waist and, laughing together, they hurried into the bathroom.

* * * *

Later, in his condo, Alex wondered how long he should wait until he felt it might be safe to ask Blake to move in with him. He hated this bit about having to leave because either he or Blake had to be up early in the morning. Mostly Blake and his office meetings. They were important of course, but wouldn't it be so much nicer if they lived together, and he could see Blake off after getting him off, of course, then coffee and maybe even some breakfast together?

Yes, it had only been a few days since their reunion, but deep inside him, he knew he was going to do his level best to make this work between them again. And he was sure it was what Blake wanted too.

They were so good together, and not just in bed, although their last bout of lovemaking before he'd left had come close to making him feel that the earth had moved at the moment of climax. He knew it had just been the bed's box-springs, but it had been so real, so all-consuming. His lips still tingled from the pressure of Blake's mouth on his, and it was difficult to erase from his mind the way everything else in the universe had shrunk down until it was just the two of them, alone in the cosmos.

He shook his head at his crazy thoughts that he hadn't dared share with Blake. He didn't want Blake to think that the man who'd come back into his life was some kind of airhead. But it was romantic, wasn't it? Maybe Blake would appreciate the analogy…

His gaze fell on the unopened mail from the day before, still on the kitchen counter where he'd left it.

He sifted through the envelopes stopping at one that was obviously from an attorney's office. "Huh…" It was postmarked Bakerton, Virginia, and a cold shiver coasted down Alex's spine. This could not be good news, or any kind of news he wanted from the town he'd left years ago. For a moment he considered throwing it in the trash, unopened, but then curiosity got the better of him and he tore the envelope open.

From: Atherton, Johnson and Straub,
Attorneys-at-Law
12 Brennen Ave., Bakerton, Va.
Dear Mr. Martin, it is our sad duty to inform you that your mother, Charlene Martin, passed away on Oct 14th 2021. Your father, Harold Martin has informed us that, despite your past differences, he would be obliged if you would attend the funeral of your late mother and consult with him at The Mercy Home for the Elderly about your future as the only remaining member of the family.

The date, time and place of the services in memory of your mother are October 31st 2022, at 3pm and will be held at The Church of Abiding Love in Bakerton, Virginia.

Please contact us for further information.
Sincerely, Henry Atherton.

Alex stared at the letter for many long moments, unable to believe what the actual fuck he was reading. *The man has the fucking audacity to contact me after all these years, to tell me that the woman who never liked me, never mind loved me, has passed and he expects me to attend her funeral. That mother fu —*

For a moment he thought his head might explode from the anger that filled him. He gripped the edge of the counter to stop himself from rampaging across the living room floor in a senseless quest for something to punch. *Not the wall*, he told himself as he stared at it in a blind fury. Chances were he'd break his fist, and his father was not worth one iota of pain, never mind the cost of repairing the plaster.

"Goddamn him!"

The piercing ring of his cell startled him. *Blake*. Oh God, he couldn't talk to him right now. *I'll most likely have a screaming fit if I start telling him about this letter.* But Blake was always so calm, so sensible. Perhaps he'd help him climb down from this mountain of rage that swelled within him.

"Hey there, beautiful." Blake's voice was low and sexy. "Just wanted to make sure you got home okay, and tell you goodnight."

"Blake." He knew his voice, by contrast, sounded decidedly unsteady. More like a croak than a voice really.

"What's wrong? You sound weird."

"My mother died."

"Oh, I'm sorry."

"Don't be, I'm not."

"*Alex.*"

"I'm not sorry, Blake. I hope you'll understand when I say I'm not in the least bit sorry or upset."

"Well, yes, I know there was no love lost between you and your parents, but, Alex…"

"There's no *but, Alex*, Blake. That bitch sent me away to suffer for close to five years in a place that could've driven me mad, or to kill myself, and now my father wants me to come to her funeral and to talk about my future. That's what I'm upset about. Fucking angry about. *My* future, Blake, like it would have anything to do with him. I have lived my life pretty damn well without either of them. Without him even wondering where the hell I was or what I was doing — and Blake, I was good with that.

"I didn't want him or my mother fucking up my life again. Hell, I don't think I could even have looked at them, never mind talk to them. I know I must sound cold but they're a part of my past I want to forget, and I had more or less. And now this. And get this, he said that *despite our past differences* he wants me at the funeral. *Past differences* sounds like we had a petty argument about the weather forecast or something, not that he had me locked up for five years of my fucking life!"

"I'm guessing you're not going to the funeral."

Alex snorted. "You couldn't be more right about that."

"How'd he know how to get in touch with you?"

"Through some attorneys. The price of being somewhat well-known." He sighed. "I'm looking at the letter, Blake, and where she's being buried is called The Church of Abiding Love. Abiding Love, Blake. The irony is almost laughable."

"You want me to come over?" Blake asked.

"No, it's late, and you have an early morning meeting. I'm a big boy and I can handle this, but I appreciate the offer."

"If you're sure."

"I'm sure. Go to bed, Blake. I'll see you tomorrow night?"

"Of course. Come over, and I'll make you some dinner. You can be dessert."

Alex smiled, hoping Blake could hear it in his voice when he said, "I can't wait. Love you, Blako." There he'd said it. Too late to take it back now.

His smile grew wider when Blake said softly, "Love you too."

"Then that's all that matters."

Chapter Eleven

The first thing Alex remembered on waking the following morning after a mostly restless and sleepless night was the letter from his father's attorneys. And dammit if that wasn't what he wanted furthest from his mind. He groaned and buried his face in his pillow.

Think of Blake instead, he told himself. *Think of the fantastic night we had together, how amazing, how incredible our love making was, and how you can't wait to do it again, and again tonight.*

His cell chimed, and he reached for it to peer still bleary-eyed at the screen. A text from Blake. That was all it took to make him feel ten times better.

Good morning, sunshine, hope you slept well.

So-so. How about you?

Like a log, and I'm hard as one.

I'll be right over.

LOL. Just kidding. I'm at the office.

Already? He glanced at his watch. Shit. It was already nine o'clock, and he had to be at the gallery at ten.

It's nine, Alex. Didn't you have a meeting with Doreen?

Yes. Sorry, I have to jump in the shower and caffeinate before I leave. I'll text you later.

Don't forget about tonight.

As if. Bye, love you.
There was a slight pause then Alex breathed a sigh of relief when Blake texted, *Love you too.*

In the shower, Alex wondered if Blake had thought any more about fostering Joey. *Maybe I should've been more encouraging. Instead of just saying I'd help, I should suggest that we'd foster the boy together. They could move into my condo. It's bigger, which would be a point in our favor. Blake's apartment is maybe too small for foster requirements.*

While he toweled off, he decided he'd mention it to Blake when they met later in the day.

* * * *

Doreen looked excited about something when he met her at the gallery a few minutes after ten.

"Sorry I'm late," he said, entering her office.

"No problem. Coffee?"

"Please."

She got up and poured him a mugful from her coffee maker. "I had a very good phone call last night. I was going to call you, but it was late. And I figured you and Blake… Well, you know." She waved her hands about as if in explanation.

Alex grinned. "Very subtle, Doreen. As a matter of fact, I slept at home last night."

"Alone?"

"Very much alone. Blake had an early morning meeting so I left him so he could get some shut-eye."

"I should think he needed it." Doreen cackled behind her hand.

Alex rolled his eyes. "You were telling me about a phone call."

"Oh, yeah. Oliver Stevenson. He owns a gallery in Frisco. The exhibition that was planned to start in two weeks has fallen through. The artist had a change of heart, or something. Oliver sounded pissed so I didn't press for details, but he wants to book you instead when you're done here. He said he'd heard and read glowing reviews of your exhibition here."

"Oh, that's great. Did he say for how long?"

"A month, but he wants you to hold the two weeks following open, just in case you're wildly popular, which I told him you were."

Alex kissed her on the cheek. "You are good for my ego."

"I wouldn't say it if 'tweren't so." She smiled sweetly. "You have another week here then we'll get you packed up and on your way. I'll come up for the day you open and stick around for a couple of days in case you need me. Maybe Blake can visit?"

"I'll ask, but…" *Shit, he might be up to his eyes with the foster application, and I won't be here to help. Damn.*

"What's wrong, honey?"

"Oh, just something Blake and I were planning."

"Getting married already?" She widened her eyes when Alex didn't scoff at the idea. "Wait, are you?"

"No, no. It's just that Blake's got himself attached to this kid, Joey, from an abusive home. The matron at the care center has talked to him about fostering Joey but he's hesitant because he's only got a one-bedroom apartment. Something that wouldn't look good apparently on his application, so I was going to suggest they move in with me, but I haven't done that yet, and now with me being out of town for maybe six weeks or so. Shit, I don't know how he'll feel about that."

Doreen frowned. "The Frisco gallery is a big deal, Alex."

"I know, and I'm sure Blake will understand that, but I feel bad about leaving him to deal with the foster thing alone."

"Honey, he's a grown man and a civil rights attorney. He'll manage just fine without you."

"Ouch. Would you mind rephrasing that?"

"You know what I mean. Besides, you have another week here, enough time to get things straightened out."

"I hope so." He just wasn't at all sure how Blake would take this news. "I got a letter from an attorney yesterday telling me my mother had passed."

"Oh. Guess I should say I'm sorry, but I know better." She knew how he felt about his parents, and Alex appreciated that she didn't express a phony sentiment. "Will there be a funeral?"

"Oh yeah, but I'm not going. My father wants me to, and to talk about my future."

Doreen gasped. "What?"

"My reaction too. After all these years he has the nerve to try and interfere with my life, as if he ever had any part in it."

"What are you going to do?"

"Call the attorney's office so they can let him know that I have no intentions of attending the funeral or of talking to him about my future or any other goddam thing." Alex held back the anger that threatened to surface again. "Or, let him know that I found the boy he locked me away from all those years ago, and we've picked up where we left off, and I've never been happier, and that conversion therapy he paid for didn't work. I'm still a homo and in love with a wonderful guy. And there's not a damned thing he can do about it."

"Wow." Doreen sounded shocked and amused at the same time. "I think I'd pay good money to witness that."

Alex snorted. "So would I, but I've got better things to do than fester over something that won't ever change. The man's been dead to me for years. I thought I was to him too, and now this. Whatever this is. Trying to salve his conscience I guess, but I can't forgive and forget that easily."

Doreen took his hand in hers. "I don't blame you, Alex. I can't begin to imagine the hell you went through being thrown out of your home then spending all those years in that god-awful institution. You've done amazingly well in spite of it all, and this is your time to shine. Shall I call Oliver Stevenson and tell him you'll be delighted to exhibit at his gallery?"

"Yes, and thank you, Doreen."

"My pleasure, honey."

* * * *

Blake glanced at his cell's screen as it vibrated on top of his desk. *Keren from Social Services.* "Hi, Keren, how are you?"

"Good, Blake, and I have news I know you'll be happy about."

"Oh yeah? Do tell."

"Well, I know you were concerned about making sure Joey Carmichael's next foster home would be a safe and happy place for him, and I've found the perfect family for him. Trudy and Bill Davis."

"Oh…" Blake knew his enthusiasm level must have sounded off, but the pang of disappointment that had hit his stomach wouldn't let him sound any other way. "Oh, that's, that's good, all right," he managed to add.

"Yes, they're friends of mine, been married two years. I was Trudy's maid-of-honor, as a matter of fact. They have a darling little house in a new development in West Covina. Trudy's husband Bill has a good steady job with the city."

"They have other kids?"

"No, Trudy can't have children, sad to say. They mentioned adoption to me about a year ago. Anyway, I showed them Joey's picture, and they can't wait to meet him. I'm sure they'll love him, and we won't have to worry about him being mistreated anymore."

"Well, he's an easy one to love." Blake told himself to get a grip and act as if he was pleased with Keren's news, for despite his feeling of loss, really this was for the best. A married couple, stable, and ready to start a family. It was ideal, and he'd just have to get over the dismay of not seeing Joey again.

"He is, isn't he," Keren was saying. "Bill and Trudy will meet him later this afternoon and if it works out, we can begin the process. I can help speed it up so that he'll soon be in a loving home."

"Yes, that's what he needs, a loving home." *He'd have had it with me and Alex, but I guess it just wasn't meant to be.* He sighed. "Well, thanks for letting me know, Keren."

After saying goodbye and disconnecting the call, he sank back in his chair and tried not to feel let down by the news. Joey would be well looked after, of that he was sure, a much better environment for him than a busy attorney he'd only see for a few hours a day, spending most of his time in daycare or kindergarten. No, this was better.

I'll convince myself of it in time.

Checking his watch, he wondered if Alex would be through with his meeting by now. Maybe they could meet for lunch. The evening suddenly seemed so far away before he'd see Alex.

God, when did I become so needy? Since meeting Alex again, that's when. He picked up his phone and punched in Alex's number.

"Hey, this is a nice surprise."

Blake couldn't help but smile on hearing the warmth in Alex's voice. That warmth seemed to find its way inside Blake and his heart thrummed from it. Wow, I'm a goner, he thought.

"Hi, Alex. You available for lunch?"

"Can't wait to see me, huh?"

Blake chuckled. "Something like that."

"Okay, how about one o'clock at Sammy's on Eighth? You know it?"

"Yes. One is good."

"Excellent. See you then. Wait, this doesn't take the place of the dinner you promised me, does it?"

"No, silly. Just think of it like it's a bonus. You getting to see me earlier, that is."

Alex laughed. "Gotcha. See you later."

* * * *

Sammy's was busy, but they managed to get a table after only a few minutes' wait. "I have something to tell you," Alex said, rubbing the side of Blake's hand with his thumb as the hostess directed them to a booth.

"Something good, I hope."

"Well, yes and no. I've been booked for a new exhibition in San Francisco, but I have to leave town for a few weeks, so that's not good."

"No, it's not," Blake agreed while taking a seat opposite Alex. "I'll miss you, but congratulations. You have to be excited."

They took the menus handed them then laid them on the table. "It's kind of a big deal," Alex said. "But without a doubt, I'll miss you too. I thought I'd have some free time after I'm through here. Time to spend with you and Joey, if you go ahead with fostering him."

"Unfortunately, that's off the table," Blake told him. "Got a call from the social worker. She's found a home for him. They sound like nice people, friends of hers as a matter of fact, so although I'm bummed, I know it's for the best for Joey, and that's what counts in the end. After all, it's his welfare I'm concerned about, and from what Keren, the social worker, told me, he's found a good home."

"Yeah, but I'm sorry it didn't pan out." Alex covered Blake's hand with his. "I know you were thinking hard about making it work, but..." He paused for a moment.

"If you want to adopt a kid, boy or girl, down the road, we could, together, I mean."

"Something to drink, guys?" The busboy's question interrupted whatever Blake was going to say. Alex noticed his badge said his name was Kevin.

"Uh, iced tea, please," Blake told him.

"And for me, Kevin." Alex gave the boy his killer smile that made him blush.

"You seducer, you," Blake said when the kid had gone. "You work that charm so well."

"As long as it works on you, that's all I care about." He stroked Blake's hand before letting go and sitting back. "I'm sorry about the time away, but it's a good gig. The guy who owns the gallery, Oliver Stevenson, is well known and his opinions are generally taken as gold."

"That's great."

"You think you could maybe come up for the weekend?"

Blake nodded. "Looks like the weeks ahead are clear apart from work. Now that Joey's gonna be well taken care of, I can relax, I guess, and not worry about him. I still feel a bit of a wrench, but inside, I know it's for the best. I was letting my emotions take control and not thinking about the reality of caring for a child. But if you're serious about what you said earlier, about us both adopting together, down the road, I'd be all up for that."

The busboy cleared his throat while he delivered their drinks. "Um, Jen's real busy so she asked me to take your order. Have you decided?"

"Yes, I'll have the house club on wheat, please, Kevin," Alex said with another big smile.

"That sounds good." Blake looked up at Kevin. "I'll have the same, thank you."

Kevin gazed at them both as if transfixed for a long moment before he mumbled, "Be right back with those," then fled.

"I think he likes you." Alex winked at Blake. "Should I be jealous?"

"You bet. He's just my type, or will be in about ten years."

Alex grinned. "So, is it too soon to ask you to move in with me?"

"Wow." Blake stared at him wide-eyed. "That came out of left field."

"Funny, to me, it's like I've waited twenty years to ask you that."

"Would you really have asked me that twenty years ago?"

"More like I'd have asked if I could come and live at your folks' house. I always preferred your place to mine. Your mom and dad were so easy to be around, so loving to you, and each other. Something I never saw from my parents."

"Mom and Dad loved you too, Alex."

"Yeah, I think they did. So what's your answer? I was going to ask you when you were considering fostering Joey and you said your place was too small. But I still want you with me, regardless of that. You don't have to say yes right now. I'll be gone for about four weeks. Six, if the option's picked up. Is that enough time for you to decide?"

"Jeez, I hate the idea of you being gone for that long. I've just got used to having you a few miles away, and now? Shit, I'll miss you." Blake rolled his eyes. "Hope I don't sound too whiny." He leaned back in his seat when Kevin arrived at their table with two large plates which he set down in front of them.

"Anything else I can get you guys?"

"Nope, looks good, Kevin, thanks," Alex said. Kevin nodded and left. Alex gazed at Blake for a few seconds then asked, "So you'll think about my offer...to move in with me, I mean?

Blake nodded. "It is a bit soon, but I think we'd be good together. When you come back from San Francisco, we can talk more about it. And I'd have to give notice at my place."

"Of course." He picked up his glass of iced tea. "So here's to the future us, Blako, living together. Cheers!"

"Cheers." Blake touched his glass to Alex's. "Here's to our future...and Joey's."

Chapter Twelve

Blake called Estelle at the care center later that afternoon. "Hi, Estelle. Keren tells me she's found a great home for Joey. Friends of hers."

"Yes, she's here with them right now." Estelle was keeping her voice low. "They're talking to Joey in my office. I just stepped out when I saw it was you on the line."

"Oh, sorry to interrupt. Uh…" He hated to put her on the spot by asking her opinion of the couple, but he figured she was a good judge of character. "Is Joey all right?"

"I don't think he understands what's goin' on, the sweet boy, but he's not being awkward or anything. Just sittin' there, listening. The Davises seem like a nice enough couple, and I think they're quite taken with Joey."

"That's good. Keren said she could speed the process up so he should have a good home in a couple of weeks."

"Or sooner. Keren's going to ask the board's approval so Joey can stay with them while the application and inspections are bein' done."

"That's good, I guess." He hesitated then asked, "You think I could come see him before he leaves the center? I'd just like to give him a hug and wish him a happy life."

"Oh…" Estelle sounded sad. "I really do wish it had been you bein' his daddy. The little boy loves you, but I guess it wasn't meant to be. Why don't you come by around five to tell him goodbye?"

"I'll be there." After they'd ended the call, Blake texted Alex and asked if he'd like to join him at the center.

Alex texted back, *No, Blake, go have your time with the kid. I know how much this means to you, to you both, so I'll just hang back, let you say your goodbyes.*

Okay, see you my place at six.

You bet you will. An emoji face appeared with hearts for eyes.

"Love you too," Blake whispered.

* * * *

Joey's eyes were as big as saucers when Blake showed up. "Brako," he yelled and flung himself into Blake's arms when Blake crouched down to catch him. Estelle let out a sigh, and even Spencer refrained from rolling his eyes when Blake stood and swung Joey high over his head. It wasn't until the shrieks of Joey's laughter had died down and he was curled up against

Blake's chest that Blake saw Keren staring at him, her expression anything but cordial. A young couple stood at her side. They didn't look too happy either.

Shit, I thought they'd have gone by now! "Oh hi, Keren." He put Joey on the ground, but the little guy immediately wrapped his arms around Blake's left leg.

"Just dropped in to tell Joey how glad I am he's found a good home." He tried to take a step toward Keren and the couple, but Joey held on tighter. "Uh, you must be Mr. and Mrs. Davis." He extended his hand, and Mr. Davis took it, but the handshake was brief.

"Looks like you have a fan," Davis said, frowning at the back of Joey's head.

"Uh, yeah…" He peeled Joey off his leg and set him in front of the Davises. "Sorry to interrupt. Nice meeting you both." He swallowed a gulp as he took in Keren's and Trudy Davis' hard stares. "Bye, Estelle."

He walked quickly to the door but not fast enough to avoid hearing Joey's wail of dismay. *Oh, man, have I ever screwed up.*

* * * *

"Why the heck didn't Estelle tell you Keren and the couple were there when you went by to see Joey?" Alex was angry for Blake being upset. "You could've gone tomorrow. I bet the kid was confused by the whole thing."

"Yeah, he was crying when I left. I feel bad for him, but also for the Davises. They didn't need to see Joey climbing all over me. I called Keren to apologize but it went to voice mail. I didn't leave a message because I want to talk to her, make sure she understands that I really regret what happened. A message just seems kind of impersonal, you know?"

Alex stroked Blake's shoulders then massaged them. "You're so tense. It wasn't your fault. You mustn't feel guilty about wanting to tell the kid goodbye. Keren knows how fond of you Joey is, and I'm sure she took care of the situation."

"It would've been better if I hadn't gone there today, though. I bet it took some time to calm Joey down."

Alex stepped away to open the bottle of wine he'd brought. He poured Blake a healthy amount. "Here, take a swig of this. It'll help calm *you* down."

"Thanks." Blake took a long sip. "I'm glad you're here."

Alex kissed his cheek. "Nowhere else I'd rather be." He poured himself a glass of wine. "Cheers." He touched his glass to Blake's. "So, what's for dinner?"

"I got some fresh salmon and a salad from the market. Hope that's okay."

"Oh, yes." He took Blake's hand and led him over to the couch, pulling him down beside him. "Wine and kisses first. You need some TLC to bring back that sunny smile of yours."

"Sunny smile?" Blake caressed Alex's cheek. "You're the one with the smile that lights up a room. Mine is more…uh, uncertain."

"No, it's not." He leaned and took Blake's lips with a long and sensuous kiss. "Mmm…" He sat back licking his lips. "You taste of apples and pears and the smoky undertones of oak."

Blake snickered. "You read the label on the wine bottle, didn't you?"

"I confess, but you do taste all kinds of delicious." He opened the top buttons of Blake's shirt and nuzzled his neck.

Blake squirmed against him and whispered, "I think I should take you to my bed, don't you?"

"Absolutely. Drink up and lead the way."

They downed their wine then Blake stood, offered Alex his hand then led him into the bedroom. Blake unbuttoned Alex's shirt then slipped his hands inside, caressing the warm, smooth skin. He shivered slightly from the sensation.

Alex smiled and leaned in for a kiss, gentle, almost shy at first, and Blake wondered at the tentativeness. "Sometimes," Alex murmured, his lips still on Blake's, "I think maybe this is all too good to be true. You and me, I mean. You in my arms, kissing me..."

"Well, to be exact, it's you kissing me right now, but keep going."

Alex growled and pressed his lips more firmly against Blake's, pushing his tongue into Blake's mouth when he opened to him. Blake moaned and crushed Alex's body to his, grinding his swollen erection against the hardness behind Alex's fly. Their kiss, a far cry from that first gentle touch, was fierce, almost bruising. They fell onto the bed, pulling at each other's clothes, and kicking off their shoes. When they were naked, they rolled across the bed together, then stilled. Blake, on top, gazed silently into Alex's eyes.

"What are you thinking?" Alex asked.

"About what you said earlier. About feeling that this is somehow too good to be true." He brushed his lips over Alex's. "But I know that, for me, this is good and right and everything I've always wanted. You, Alex.

Without even knowing it, I've been waiting for you. You truly are unforgettable."

"And that's how I feel about you, Blako. When I was at Farmton, I thought about you all the time, wondered how you were, what you were doing. I planned to escape just to get to you, thinking crazy thoughts like your folks would take me in and hide me from the authorities and my parents. Nuts, right?"

"I'm sure they would've done their best for you. You could've stayed in my room."

"And here I am, twenty years later, in your room." He smiled. "And in your bed."

"Where you belong." Blake kissed his lips, his jaw, his neck, his chest, drawing each tiny nipple into his mouth, licking and nipping at them, loving the moaning sounds escaping from Alex's throat.

"Turn over," he said his voice low and husky, and Alex immediately complied, raising his pretty ass in invitation. Blake kissed his nape then ran his tongue the length of Alex's spine. He kissed Alex's right ass cheek then the left, lingering over the firm smooth flesh, feeling Alex shiver.

"Blake," he whispered.

"You have a beautiful ass," Blake murmured before nestling between Alex's butt cheeks, using the tip of his tongue to circle then probe at Alex's pulsing hole. He pressed forward, giving Alex's entrance a long, deep lick, and Alex, a whimper tearing loose from his lips, arched upward, pushing his butt into Blake's searching tongue as if demanding more. Blake spread Alex's cheeks with the palms of his hands to get better access to that sweet pucker then he was fucking Alex with his tongue. Alex squirmed under Blake, groaning from the shivering ecstasy Blake knew he was experiencing. He added a finger alongside his tongue, curling it around Alex's prostate and Alex yelled, "Blake, oh my god, Blake!"

Blake smiled at his lover's reaction. He slid up Alex's back, kissing his spine all the way up to his neck. "You like that?" he whispered into the shell of Alex's ear.

"Oh God, yes. Never had that before."

"Never?"

Alex turned onto his back and met Blake's eyes. "I guess I should've told you I am probably the most inexperienced guy you've ever been with."

"Hard to believe, someone who looks like you." Blake kissed his lips. "And has such a delectable ass."

"That wants more than just your tongue inside it." Alex's eyes gleamed with unrestrained lust. "Fuck me, Blake. I need you all the way inside me."

Blake grabbed the necessaries wishing that they could go bare. "Have you been tested recently?"

"About six months ago. Doctor's orders. I was neg, and I haven't had sex with anyone since then." He bit his lip. "Or before really." *Only with Cody and that wasn't what either of us really wanted....* "How about you?"

"No sex since my last boyfriend. I got tested after we split just to be sure and that was a year ago. Told you I'm a slow mover. You wanna go bare?"

"Not so slow then." Alex smiled. "I'd love it. You inside me without any latex in between. Sounds like heaven."

"It does, doesn't it." He squirted some lube onto his fingertips and started to prep Alex.

"Mmm..." Alex bore down on Blake's fingers, drawing him in, clenching down tight. "Love it so far."

Blake kissed him as he pulled out then pushed his erection against Alex's quivering hole, penetrating him with slow, sure thrusts, savoring the sensation of Alex's hot flesh enveloping his naked, rock-hard erection.

"Oh, my God," he whispered on a gasp of elation. "Feels so good, Alex. You are beautiful inside and out."

Alex writhed under him, tightening his legs around Blake's waist, his arms around his neck, holding him in place while he pressed kiss after kiss on Blake's mouth, his jaw, his neck.

"Blake," he gasped in between kisses. "This is amazing. I never knew it would be so incredible. You're perfect in there. God, I can actually feel you pulsing inside me. Now give it to me, *hard*. Fuck me, Blake!"

"You got it." Blake pulled out halfway then rammed himself back inside Alex, quickening the pace, their bodies slamming together when Alex met every one of Blake's powerful thrusts, straining his hips upward, matching Blake's almost frantic rhythm.

Sweat coated their bodies, and dripped from Blake's forehead onto Alex's lips where it was quickly licked up. Alex stared up at him, a wanton desire etched in his gleaming blue eyes, darkened now by lust. He clung to Blake as if he were his lifeline, gasping, moaning, panting out words that didn't make a lot of sense but that urged Blake on to the edge of orgasm. He grasped Alex's throbbing erection marveling again at the silk-like texture that covered the rigid flesh. Everything about Alex was just so fucking incredible.

"So close," Alex whispered, and Blake covered his mouth with a searing kiss that took them both over the edge. Alex gave a joyful shout as he came, his cum jetting between their torsos. Blake, shuddering from the power of his orgasm, managed one last ramming thrust deep inside Alex before choking out a cry of triumph. He was held in a rib-crushing embrace by his lover who crooned Blake's name over and over ending with "I love you, I love you, I love you…"

Blake swore he had never been happier in his life. Even that amazing moment when he and Alex had been reunited faded in comparison to the way he felt now. In those twenty years they'd been apart, he yearned, hoped and wished for this, but had never believed it would happen. And here they were, locked in an embrace he'd only dreamed about.

"I love you too, Alex. Always have, always will."

He lay over Alex, returning the kisses his lover showered on him, until they calmed, and he basked in the euphoria that enveloped him.

"Mmm…" Alex squirmed around Blake's cock that was still deep within him. "That was amazing, feeling you come inside me, I mean. So hot and powerful. I want to hold your cum inside me forever. You're still hard. Maybe we could go again?"

Blake chuckled. "Maybe, if you give me a half-hour or so. I feel a doze coming on."

Alex yawned. "Yeah, not a bad idea. Then after, we can go again."

Chapter Thirteen

Blake called Keren the following morning. His night with Alex had been fantastic as always and had helped take the edge off his worry that he had somehow screwed up Joey's chances of being fostered by good people.

"Hey, Keren, it's Blake Carson." The voice mail message he'd listened to had irritated him. He wanted to apologize but not on some digital piece of technology that would be unable to convey the sincerity of his apology. He liked Keren and didn't want their professional relationship damaged in any way.

"Listen, I…" *Hurry up, dummy, before the beep cuts you off.* "Uh, I wanted to say sorry for that scene at the care center yesterday. I just stopped in to say goodbye to Joey and wish him well, but you know what an exuberant kid he is. Anyway, I hope your friends weren't upset by me being there and that they haven't changed their minds about fostering Joey. He for sure needs a good home, and, well, that's it. Give me a call when you have the time, and again, I'm sorry."

He sat back in his chair and sighed. He couldn't help but wonder what the fallout, if any, had been. Had Joey given vent to a tantrum, and the Davises had decided he wasn't the little angel they wanted in their home? Joey could be difficult, but couldn't all children be from time to time? And he really was a sweet kid. They must have seen that when he was in their company. He'd give Keren another call later.

He looked up as Roger, their senior partner, entered his office after a brief knock. "Blake, I've got a new case for you. You have time to look at the file with me?"

"Of course." Blake would be glad to have something to take his mind off Joey, Keren and the Davises, if only for a few hours.

Keren called him just before he left the office, and he breathed a sigh of relief when she told him everything was okay, and the Davises were going ahead with the foster application.

"I knew Joey was very fond of you," she said, "and I explained that to Trudy and Bill and they were okay with it. They know Joey's been through a rough time, and it was Bill who said he could understand an abused kid gravitating to someone who showed him affection."

"Well, I'm glad that worked out, and again I'm sorry I just dropped in at the center without letting you know first. Was he okay once I'd left?"

"He took a little time to calm down, but Trudy is good with kids and that helped a lot."

"That's great. I'm sure Joey will love having a good home. It's what he needs to get over the trauma of living with the Harrises."

"Absolutely. Okay, Blake, I'm sure we'll be working together again at some point."

"Sad, but true. No offense, of course."

"None taken. I know what you mean. If you like, I can keep you up-to-date with his progress."

"I'd like that very much."

"Okay, will do. Take care, Blake. Bye."

"Bye, Keren."

* * * *

The week slipped by too fast for Blake's liking. Alex would be leaving for San Francisco in a couple of days now that his exhibition was over in LA. He'd had to spend a lot of his time arranging the packing and shipping of his work and their time together had been limited. Blake told himself not to get upset, but he'd become so used to seeing Alex every day for the past close to three weeks that his absence left Blake off-kilter and feeling somehow depleted.

Shit, what's it going to be like when he's gone for a whole month or longer? And San Francisco – the gayest city in America. What if he meets someone up there that more than just interests him? Okay, now you're being paranoid, but he is a gorgeous man and bound to catch many an eye. Many a lust-filled eye. Damn!

You really need to get a grip, Mr. Needy. It isn't like I don't know anyone else in LA.

He had a couple of friends he saw on a fairly regular basis, Patrick and Mark from his internship days, and now when he thought about it, he hadn't called them since he and Alex had been dating. Maybe he could arrange to have them meet Alex sometime soon.

His cell chimed, signaling an incoming text.

Hi, handsome, you available for dinner? Thought I'd take you out on the town.

What town?

Ha ha. How about Lucky's in Pasadena, then you can come spend the night with me. Last chance before I leave so I advise you not to miss this fantastic opportunity.

Blake grinned. *Fantastic huh? I better up my game.*

Your game is perfect. So 7 at Lucky's?

I'll be there. Ciao, babe.

Hasta la vista, muchacho!

Blake grinned and glanced at his watch. His three o'clock would be arriving in about twenty minutes. A young gay married couple who'd just bought a condo in Belmont and were suffering from homophobic neighbors. They had complained to the homeowners' association, but no one on the board wanted to confront the bigots and told the guys to just ignore the taunts and name calling. Now they wanted to sue, and Blake couldn't blame them. How galling to have bought their first home together and end up with this kind of creepy neighbors. Blake was certainly going to do his best for them.

Dale and Henry Bloomfield were a charming couple, good-looking in an unassuming way and with shy manners that made Blake think of a bygone age when everyone was polite to one another. They gave Blake a brief background of the problem.

"I think in a way it was my fault," Dale explained, his brown eyes sad in his earnest expression. "We wanted to be good neighbors, so we went out of our way to be friendly with the Herriots, June and Fred, and they were okay in the beginning. Then one day Fred saw me kissing Henry goodbye on my way to work and he almost imploded right in front of us. Called us names I'd never heard before. I tried to calm him down, but he ran from us, yelling at the top of his voice, then slammed the door to his place so loud, other neighbors came out to see what the fuss was about."

"It wasn't your fault, Dale," Henry said, patting Dale's arm. "We were still inside our condo, the door was open, but he must have been peering around the corner in order to see us. Nosy old so-and-so." He gave Blake an appealing look. "But, Mr. Carson, we want him stopped. He's making our lives miserable, and we can't just up and sell so soon after buying. We'd lose money we can't afford to."

"What about the wife? Does she get involved in the harassment?"

"Not really, but she doesn't try to stop it."

"And has he gotten violent?"

"Just verbally." Dale rolled his eyes. "You should hear the vitriol that comes pouring out of his mouth every time he sees us. Religious stuff, hell and brimstone, us on the Devil's spit. Stupid stuff like that, but he's never tried to shove us or anything like that. Sometimes I wish he would, so I could deck him."

"That's all we'd need," Henry exclaimed. "The good thing is, the other neighbors don't like him and haven't sided with him. That is, except for one old dude who lives under us. But he doesn't like us for a different reason."

"What's that?"

"Well…" Henry's cheeks grew pink. "He said he can hear us in bed. We've tried to tamp it down, but you know…"

"Yeah, I do." Blake smiled. He wasn't about to fill them in on the noises he and Alex were capable of.

"He's just jealous," Dale said. "I bet he hasn't been laid in twenty years."

"*Dale.*" Henry slapped his husband's arm, not so gentle this time.

Blake laughed. "Well, what if we start with a cease-and-desist letter? A lot of times that can put an end to it. Most people don't like a letter from a lawyer's office. It can make them nervous and rethink their attitude. If that doesn't work, we'll threaten them with a harassment suit. But I do advise you to call the police the next time he gets in your faces with more of that. Hate speech isn't necessarily a hate crime, only if it leads to violence or threat of such."

"He did say he'd love to squish me, if he could get away with it," Dale told him.

"Squish you?" Blake couldn't help the chuckle that slipped from his lips. "Doesn't sound too macho."

"He's not," Henry said. "He's a skinny thing with a mouth even Roseanne Barr would envy."

"What does he do for a living?" Blake asked.

"Apart from harassing us? He's a mail delivery driver," Dale told him.

"A job he wouldn't like to lose. Hmm…" Blake gave them a conspiratorial smile. "A subtle threat in the letter might do the trick."

"Is that legal?" Henry asked.

"It is when worded correctly."

"Okay." Dale rubbed his hands together. "Let's do it!"

"I'll get right on it." Blake placed a document in front of them. "This is a legal form stating that you are being represented by Benson and Sellers, Attorneys-at-law, in this case. It requires your signatures. Then I'll send Mr. Herriot a registered cease-and-desist letter. If you get any grief from him after he receives the letter, let me know immediately and we will take the next step."

"Which is?" Henry asked.

"We'll acquire a court-approved restraining order which, if he violates, will result in his arrest."

Dale's eyes gleamed. "I like the sound of that."

Henry demurred. "I hope it doesn't come to that."

* * * *

Alex was already seated at a table in Lucky's when Blake arrived. "You look nice," he said as Blake slid into the booth opposite him.

"Thanks, I had time to go home, shower and change before getting here."

"Perhaps nice isn't the word to describe you." Alex sent him a sex-filled leer wrapped up in a smile. "More like delicious, or even yummy. You have that, I want to lick you all over right now look. And talking of that, I have something to show you. Some *things* actually." He picked up a large envelope Blake hadn't noticed from the seat beside him. Opening it, he handed Blake what looked like a portfolio.

"What's this?"

"Open it."

Blake lifted the cover. "Oh wow, who's this guy?"

"You, dummy."

"Oh, the day in the park. Wow," he said again as he turned picture after picture over. "I, I never knew I looked so…"

"Beautiful?"

"Well, I wouldn't go that far, but you have made me seem, *better*, I guess is the word."

"Beautiful is the word, Blake. You are all that, and it's not skin deep. There's a glow about you that comes through and is extremely photogenic."

"Glow is right. My face is burning right now. You say the darnedest things." Blake smiled when he came to the last photo. It was the selfie Alex had taken with his phone. "We look happy."

"I'm happy, Blake. Are you?"

"Very. Just thinking about you makes me feel that way. Among other things."

Alex winked. "Too bad we're stuck in a restaurant where the patrons might take exception to my flagrant display of PDA, or PDL."

"What's the L stand for?"

"Lust, Blako. Sheer, unadulterated lust."

"Wow." Blake shivered for dramatic effect. "I think I'm being ravished right where I sit." He grinned. "You do that so well."

"Can I help it if ravishing you, or even better, you ravishing me is all I think of twenty-four-seven? What d'you want to drink?" he added quickly as a waiter approached their table.

"Think I'll have a Scotch on the rocks tonight. I have a feeling I need fortification for the night ahead."

"Good idea."

"What can I bring you, gentlemen?" the waiter, whose badge said his name was Karl, asked with a flirty smile.

"Two Scotches on the rocks, please." Alex returned his smile.

"Comin' right up."

"I think he likes you," Alex said after the guy had gone.

"You always say that, but it's you they always smile at."

"'Cause they know they better not mess with my man."

Blake snorted. "I'm your man?"

"You better believe it. I'm gonna have you tattooed, Property of Alex Martin, in the middle of a bunch of swirls and cherubs, before I leave town."

Blake burst out laughing and was still giggling when Karl came back with their drinks.

"Must've been a good one," he remarked.

"Oh, you have no idea," Blake managed to choke out.

"I'm a wit," Alex told Karl.

"And that's only half of it," Blake said through his laughter.

"Hey." Alex tried to look offended while the waiter smiled and placed their drinks on the table.

"Can I take your food order?"

"I'll have the New York steak, medium rare, and a baked potato with everything." Alex grinned at Blake. "Gonna need all the carbs I can get so I can work 'em off later."

Blake rolled his eyes. "I'll have the same, thanks."

"Medium rare also?"

"Please."

"Very good. Be back in a few."

"So..." Alex lifted his glass. "Cheers, Blako. I'm really gonna miss you while I'm away."

Blake touched his glass to Alex's. "I'll sure miss your repartee. You'll have to text me all day with some more of your borderline embarrassing quips."

"Am I really embarrassing?"

"No, I'm just super-sensitive."

"You're just super, period." Alex reached across the table and ran his fingers over the back of Blake's hand. "Are you glad we met up again after all this time?"

"Very glad." Blake grinned at him. "But glad is like nice, not good enough to describe how I feel. I'm more, uh, gloriously happy."

"I like that. Me too, gloriously happy." He winked at Blake. "And when I take you home you can make me even happier by ravishing me for real, all night long."

Blake was very much aware of his hard-on pressing against his pants zipper. He shifted carefully to ease the pressure. "Okay, so stop with the sex talk, or we might both get escorted out of here, and right now, I don't want to stand up."

Alex grinned but stayed quiet while Karl delivered their dinners. "Enjoy, gentlemen." He gave them a slight bow then left.

It was obvious Alex couldn't wait to spit out what he had to say. "I saw an old movie once where a guy got serviced by someone who'd crawled under the table. You think anyone would notice if I did that?"

Blake almost choked on the piece of steak he'd just popped into his mouth. "Yes, Alex, *everyone* would notice. Now cut it out till I get you home. The ravishing has to wait."

"Spoilsport," Alex mumbled. "Okay," he said, chewing happily. "Change of subject. How'd your day go?"

"I have a couple of new clients, gay guys, married, being harassed by a homophobic neighbor in the condo building they just bought into."

"Shit, what's wrong with people? What happened to live and let live?"

"A philosophy the neighbor's never heard of, from the way he's been acting," Blake said. "Nothing violent, just verbal insults, gay-baiting really, but it's making the guys very uncomfortable."

"I bet. Think I'd be punching the fucker on the nose."

"Yeah, one of the guys would love to do that too, but that can lead to bigger problems. I'm hoping a cease-and-desist letter will end it. They won't ever be friends, but the harassment should stop."

"Hope so. But isn't it crazy that they should have to put with this kind of crap in this day and age?"

"Believe me, Alex, this kind of crap is all too prevalent regardless of the day and age. Even though we have greater protections than we used to, there is still a lot of hatred out there for minorities."

"Sadly, that is true."

"But, tonight, because you're leaving tomorrow, is all about you and me, so no anger or sadness is allowed." Blake lifted his glass. "Here's to your success in San Francisco. I'm so proud of you, Alex."

"Thanks, Blake." He clinked their glasses together. "I love you."

"Love you too."

Chapter Fourteen

Blake had insisted on driving Alex to LAX for his flight to San Francisco, despite his protests that he could Uber and it would be a bitch on the freeway on the drive back.

"I get to spend some more time with you before you leave," had been Blake's reply and that settled it. Last night had been bittersweet. Their lovemaking had been exhilarating as always but tinged with the sad knowledge that the days ahead would see them separated for a while until Blake could join Alex for a weekend or so. His gallery opening was scheduled for the end of his first week there, and Doreen had told him Oliver Stevenson was pulling out all the stops to attract local art lovers and luminaries in the field of photography.

Blake pulled his car into a parking bay a safe distance from prying eyes then shut the engine off. "I need a long, long kiss before I let you go," he murmured, pulling Alex into his arms.

"And you'll get it," Alex said smiling. "What d'you reckon is the longest kiss you've ever had?"

"Well, it has to have been with you. I don't think I was as invested in longevity before you." He touched his lips to Alex's. "My ex was more of a pecker than tongues and teeth."

Alex laughed. "A pecker?"

"Yeah, you know…" He pursed his lips and placed a fast kiss on Alex's mouth.

"That's it?"

"That's it."

"Oh, my God. So how did you learn to kiss so well if that's all you were used to?"

Blake grinned. "It was all you, babe. Who wouldn't want to be inside that luscious mouth of yours?"

"Oh, Blake." He wrapped his arms around Blake's neck and pressed his parted lips to Blake's. "I am so going to miss you, sweetheart," he mumbled.

The kiss that followed was the longest Blake could ever remember, and never would forget.

On their way to the gate, they each pulled one of Alex's bags behind them and held hands for as long as they could. This parting was going to be rough, and they both knew it. Blake could tell by the way Alex's fingers tightened on his before reluctantly freeing them so he could get his boarding pass from his jacket's inside pocket. He had already checked in online, so after handing over his bags, there was nothing left to do but say goodbye. Blake could already feel the hollowness in his chest when Alex turned, slipped his arms around him and buried his face in Blake's neck.

"Come soon as you can," he whispered.

"I will, and call or text me when you land, okay?"

Alex nodded and kissed Blake's mouth. "I love you."

"Love you too. Always will."

With a sad smile Alex walked past the barrier and joined the line for security. Blake watched until he disappeared from view before he headed for the parking garage.

All the way to the office his mind was filled with thoughts of Alex and their future together. There was no doubt in his mind he wanted that future. Nor was there doubt that he was in love with Alex. Everything about the way they interacted and related to each other made him more convinced of it with each passing day. That first day in the gallery, he'd instinctively known it was Alex behind him. That's how in tune they'd been with each other, and still were.

In Blake's opinion, they fit together, both in mind and body. They shared the same kind of sense of humor. Corny jokes, and Alex loved to tease him to try and get a rise out of him, and Blake loved that, sometimes pretending to be pissed before jumping on him and tickling him unmercifully. Nobody laughed or screamed 'Uncle' louder than Alex when the tickling became unbearable.

The physical side of their relationship was golden as far as Blake was concerned and he was pretty sure Alex agreed with him if their time in bed was anything to go by. Alex's eager willingness to give himself to Blake in every possible way was more than enough evidence that Blake was doing something right, and that in itself continued to surprise and delight him. He had never considered himself sexy or a great lover—and he was sure Bradford, his ex, would agree with him about that—but Alex's reactions during their love making made him realize that to have great sex one had to have the right partner.

All these positive thoughts put him in a good mood, so he was surprised when he entered Benson and Sellers' front office, and Laura, their receptionist, gave him a grim look.

"There's a *gentleman* waiting to see you." She rolled her eyes while she emphasized the word, which to Blake meant, she thought he was a jerk.

"Where?"

She nodded toward his open office door. "In there. He wouldn't wait out here. I've been keeping an eye on him in case he started snooping."

Who the hell...?

"Thanks, Laura." He walked into the room and locked eyes with a skinny guy of about fifty who jumped to his feet, glaring at Blake as though he'd like to deck him.

"You Blake Carson?"

"I am. And you are?"

"I'm Fred Herriot, the man you sent a scurrilous letter to telling me I'd better leave those faggots alone, or else!"

Okaaay... "First of all, Mr. Herriot, do you have legal representation with you?"

"What?" Herriot's face bloomed red. "No, I don't have no *legal representation*, you uppity fuck," he yelled. "I'm here to—"

Blake held up his hand to silence him. "Without a lawyer by your side you have no business here, Mr. Herriot. I suggest you leave, or I shall call security and have you removed."

"Why you fucking ass—"

"Mr. Herriot!" Blake took a step toward the fuming man, hoping his height would be enough to intimidate the man into silence, at least. "Language like that will get you nowhere except the door." Over Herriot's shoulder, Blake could see Laura signaling frantically to someone down the hall. "Now, will you leave, or shall I call security?"

"You fucking little shit, I'll—"

Blake cut him off. "I don't think you're in a position to call anyone *little*, Mr. Herriot."

"What's going on here?"

Herriot whirled around to face the owner of the voice behind him. "Who the fuck are you?"

"I am Roger Benson, the senior partner of Benson and Sellers."

"*Benson and Sellers*," Herriot parroted in a sneering tone. "Well, you got the initials right. Fucking BS is what you're all about." Herriot pointed at Blake. "And this motherfucker sent me a letter saying that I had to lay off with *verbal attacks* on my neighbors. Like anyone would want to defend the likes of them for Chrissakes. They're faggots, and—"

Blake had had enough. "Mr. Herriot, I'm warning you for the last time. Curb your language and calm yourself down or you will be escorted from the building."

"By you? Another cocksucker? I don't think so." He lunged like a madman at Blake, who put his arm up to defend himself, and Herriot's nose connected with the bone in Blake's elbow. "Ow!" He howled and reeled back, covering his nose with his hands. Blood seeped through his fingers. "You fucking broke my nose. I'm gonna sue for this. You attacked me and broke my nose!"

"No, you attacked Mr. Carson," Benson told him, quietly. "You hit his elbow with your nose."

Blake just managed to choke back the laughter that Benson's remark invoked. He'd never heard anything funnier in his life. Benson beckoned at the security officer who loomed in the doorway.

"Come on in, Harper. Blake, call the police, and, Harper, cuff Mr. Herriot until they arrive."

"You can't do that," Herriot screeched, trying without success to struggle out the big security officer's grasp.

"Yes, we can," Benson told him. "You're being held under citizens' arrest for threatening behavior and attempted assault."

"Fucking communists, all of you!" Herriot yelled and tried to kick Harper on the shin. Harper swore under his breath as he wrenched Harriot's arms behind him and cuffed him.

Blake wasn't sure how all this would play out. Maybe when Herriot got his nose seen to and had time to cool off in a cell, he'd rethink his situation and cut out the harassment of his neighbors. Or, he'd lose it completely and make matters even worse. The police would have to be convinced to arrest him and there were plenty of witnesses to attest to Herriot's violent behavior, but in cases like this, one could never second-guess the outcome.

He watched Harper drag Herriot from his office, the man still screaming obscenities at the group of people who'd come to find out what the ruckus was all about. Laura was busy filling in everyone who'd listen about the 'madman'.

It seemed an eternity for the cops to show up. Two burly men with pissed-off expressions meant to intimidate. Roger Benson, who was still in Blake's office, waved them in and offered them seats.

"We've spoken to Mr. Herriot down in the guards' room," the older of the two said, after introducing himself and his partner as Officers Greene and Hubbard and accepting seats opposite Blake's desk. "He says he was attacked, and his nose injured by a Blake Carson."

"That's me," Blake said, "and he's lying. He made a move toward me in an antagonistic fashion, I put my arm up, like so…" Blake raised his arm to demonstrate. "And he walked into my elbow."

"With his nose," Benson added. *He's loving that part.* "It should be noted that Herriot was extremely insulting about two clients of ours, using vile language and generally making an absolute fool of himself."

"That right?" Greene didn't look too impressed, so Blake quickly outlined what had led to the scene.

"I thought the cease-and-desist letter would perhaps end his bigoted verbal attacks on our clients," Blake told them. "But instead, he saw fit to come here and threaten me and Mr. Benson."

"We are going to press charges," Benson said. "I'm not having clients of ours, nor my colleagues, threatened in anyway by some maniac who can't control his mouth or his violent nature."

The cops looked at each other as if surprised by Roger's vehemence. "You want us to arrest him?" Greene asked.

"Yes, and detain him until he has at least cooled down. I can't imagine how he might act toward his neighbors now. Surely you don't want him to harm our clients?"

"Well, there's no proof of that happening so far," Officer Hubbard said. "Now, is there?"

Roger raised his eyebrows. "But if he does act out in a violent way, you might have a hate crime on your hands. Would it not be best to avoid that happening?"

The cops exchanged looks again, then Greene sighed. "So we'll talk to him again and give him a warning to keep away from the neighbors he's allegedly harassing."

"Well, if that's the best you can do, let him know we're pressing charges, and he'd better lawyer-up," Roger snapped.

Blake eyed the cops and shook his head at their seeming indifference. "Our main concern here is for our clients and their safety. Herriot comes across as more than just a tad unhinged and after seeing him coming unglued here today, I honestly think he's capable of physical violence."

"We'll take that into consideration," Greene said and stood, Hubbard following his lead.

"What a waste," Roger muttered when the door closed behind the cops.

Blake sighed. "I'm gonna call Dale and Henry and warn them to keep their door locked tonight and to call the cops right away if Herriot tries anything over there."

Roger's cell chimed, and he answered quickly. "Oh, hi, Harper. What's the news?" He put his cell on speaker so that Blake could hear.

"We treated Herriot for his injury," Harper told them. "Good news is his nose isn't broken just bloody, but he'll have a pair of black eyes for a few days. Right now he's cussing out the cops, and they're pissed. If he doesn't shut that mouth of his, they're gonna lock him up till he cools down."

"Which is what we wanted them to do. The man's a menace."

"Oh yeah..." Harper snickered. "They're cuffing him and taking him away. Can't say I'm sorry to see the back of that one. They'll probably hold him overnight."

"That'll give me time to talk to Dale and Henry about getting a restraining order against Herriot," Blake said after Harper had hung up.

Blake sent a formal request to the LAPD for a copy of the police report regarding Fred Herriot's arrest so that he could attach it to the restraining order he'd get from the court. This would take a few days and in the meantime no doubt Herriot would be released. He didn't think for a minute that the man would listen to the police officers' warning. He was liable to go ballistic when he found out that Benson and Sellers were pressing charges of attempted assault.

Well, let him find out the hard way that the law doesn't allow for the kind of vindictive bully he is.

He put in a quick call to Dale and Henry letting them know what had transpired in his office, and to make sure they stayed away from confrontations with the idiot, and to keep their door shut and locked.

* * * *

It was strange having an evening ahead of him without Alex being a part of it. Over the past month, they'd spent almost every night together and Blake's apartment had never seemed as empty as it did now. After stripping down to his boxer briefs, he pulled a beer from the fridge then sat at the bar going over the texts he and Alex had exchanged since Alex had landed in San Francisco.

Hey lover, I'm here.

No you're there. I want you here.

Aw, miss me already?

You know I do.

Oliver met me at the airport. He seems nice.

How nice?

Just nice. Not as nice as you.

Okay then. What's the plan for today?

Hotel check in then over to Oliver's gallery for a cheese and wine or some kind of gathering.

Why did that stir unease in Blake's stomach? *Seeing a lot of Oliver then?*

I guess. He's the gallery owner. I'm more or less gonna be with him every day. Don't worry, babe, I'm yours alone.

Yeah, sorry for being stupid. I know you're mine. God, I miss you. Wanna hold you and kiss you.

You're torturing me, babe. Oh, gotta go. Later.

Later had been a call from Alex while Blake was leaving the office. Alex had sounded excited, and Blake wanted to be excited for him. He wasn't about to tell him of his confrontation with Herriot, so he'd put as much enthusiasm in his voice as he could muster, but in the end Alex had seen through his forced gusto and called him on it.

"Blako, I know this is going to be hard on both of us. We've been back together for just a few weeks and maybe this separation has come at a bad time, but believe me I'm thinking of you every minute, even when Oliver's extolling the virtues of Frisco and the gallery and the people. Yes, I'm thrilled to be a part of it all, but it's you in my heart, Blake...always, and only you."

And Blake had felt like an ass for behaving like one. "I'm sorry sweetheart. I don't want to rain on your parade. You deserve this, so I'll shut up and let you enjoy it."

"Don't shut up. Tell me that you love me."

"I love you."

"Good. I love you too, and knowing that, I can go face San Francisco's so-called elite for cheese and wine, 'cause I'll be thinking of you all the way through it."

God... When did I become so needy? Do I have to hear him say he loves me all day? Do I have to know that he's thinking of me all the time even when he's with Oliver and the gallery-goers? Yep. I do, because it tells me I have something they don't. Alex. And that's –

He was still holding his phone when it rang and it made him jump. "Hello...uh, Blake Carson here." *Jeez, what happened to my voice? I sounded like Mickey Mouse.*

"Oh hi, it's Dale Bloomfield."

"Hi, Dale. Sorry, you caught me wool-gathering."

"Really? That's cute. Anyway, thought you might be interested to know we had a visit from June Herriot a few minutes ago."

"Oh yeah? She mad that I got her hubby locked up?"

"No, she was over the moon about it." He could tell Dale was trying to hold back his mirth as he talked. "She had a suitcase with her, Blake. She said this was the opportunity she'd been waiting for, so she could walk out and get the hell away from the 'nasty little fucker'. Her words, not mine."

"Wow."

"Yeah, that was pretty much my reaction at first. I asked her to come in, and she did and said she could only stay a few minutes because she had a plane to catch. But she had time to knock back the martini Henry made for her. Seems she and Fred have been married for fifteen years and for the last two she's been looking for a way out. To get away from his 'vindictive skinny ass'. Again, her words not mine."

"Did she say where she was going?" Blake asked.

"We're sworn to secrecy, but I guess we can tell you. Cleveland, Ohio, but get this, she's going to stay with her high school sweetheart she's secretly been in touch with for the last two years."

"That's amazing! There's a major story there. I can't imagine how Fred Herriot is going to take this when he finds out."

"Scream and yell, probably. He's kinda good at that."

"Tell me about it. Anyway, I've requested a full report from the LAPD so, if necessary, we can serve him with a restraining order. And on top of that, my boss wants to press charges for his attempt to attack me, so one way or another, Fred Herriot will be tied up with legal action for a while."

"That's good. Can't think of anything he deserves more. Thanks, Blake, for all you're doing for us."

"It's my job, but I want to make sure you guys are safe, too."

"Appreciate that. G'night, Blake."

"G'night. I'll be in touch."

He went to bed that night, kind of exhausted from the drama of the day. But he couldn't sleep, and it wasn't long before he was staring at his phone's screen and pressing Alex's number so he could text him goodnight.

Having an early night so just wanted to wish you goodnight, and hope everything went well.

A few seconds later Alex texted him.

Me too. Long day. My face aches from smiling so much.

Bet you were a hit though.

Guess so.

You okay? You seem down.

No, I'm good. Just tired. I miss you and love you.

Ditto. Love you so much.

That makes it better. Night, Blake.

A string of heart emojis followed.

Night, lover.

Chapter Fifteen

Alex called him early next morning. "Sleep well?"

"Yeah, I felt better after trading texts with you. It helps to know you're within reach, even if it's by electronic means."

"Yeah, same."

"You still sound a little down," Blake said. "What's wrong?"

"Nothing I can't handle."

"What does that mean? Tell me."

"Oh, just a little miscommunication."

"Oliver put the make on you, didn't he?"

"You're too smart by half." He sighed. "Yeah, after he closed up the gallery."

"That bastard."

"Well, to be fair, I hadn't said anything about having a boyfriend, and I guess Doreen hadn't either, it's just that he didn't back off when I did tell him. It was awkward to say the least."

"If I fly up there and lay Oliver out, will that affect your exhibition?"

"Probably. Don't worry, Blake, I can handle it. I've been hit on before and survived. Besides, once he sees big and butch you, he'll know he doesn't stand a chance."

"How did you, you know, leave things?"

"I told him I wasn't interested. Funny thing is I don't think he believed me. He's a bit of a narcissist. *How could anyone ever resist me?* kind of guy. He is good-looking, but the ego is just too much. Good thing is, he did a pretty good job of displaying my work. I only had to have them move a couple of frames, and the lighting in his gallery is fantastic. So there's that."

"I hate him," Blake said.

"Are you going all alpha on me?"

"Maybe."

Alex sighed. "I've just been gone a day, and I miss you so much. Will you come up this weekend? I'm at the Hotel L'Hirondelle. It's kinda nice and it's near the gallery on Folsom Street."

"Friday night, I'll be there. I'll rent a car as it'll be late."

"I'm already excited and it's still four days away. Oh, how's that new case going? The guys being harassed by their neighbor?"

"Funny you should ask." Blake gave him a quick summary of what had happened with Herriot then ended with what Dale had told him, about the wife leaving him.

"Jeez, that all just sounds so bizarre. But the guy tried to attack you! Are you all right?"

"Yes. The way my boss tells it, Herriot hit me on my elbow with his nose."

"Oh my God."

Alex's laughter was a balm to Blake's psyche. He was still rattled about Oliver trying to hit on Alex. He wasn't sure how he'd react when he saw the creep at the gallery. For Alex's sake, of course he'd have to act as if it was no big deal, but if he got the fucker on his own, well, he could think of a few choice words that would set Oliver, the gallery owner, back on his heels.

"Okay, babe, I have to go get ready for work. Text or call me whenever you want. You know I always have time for you."

"Mmm, good to know. Love you."

"Love you too."

* * * *

Alex was less stressed after talking to Blake. Last night had been an eye-opener. One thing for sure, Oliver Stevenson could not hold his drink. Halfway through the evening, he'd gotten tipsy, which had been okay, at first. He'd been kind of amusing, flirty but not just with Alex. By the end of the party, it was a different story. He'd been downright obnoxious, pawing at Alex and trying to kiss him once they'd seen the last of the guests out. Alex had done just about everything he could, without getting mad, to avoid the groping. He'd laughed at first then resorted to light pushing to get out of the man's clutches. Finally, he'd just told the man to fuck off and left the gallery on his own.

Earlier, Oliver had asked if he'd join him at one of the many bars on Folsom, after the party. At first, Alex had been fine with that, but it soon became obvious that Oliver would prove to be a giant pain in the ass if he had anymore to drink.

Back in his hotel room, Alex had wondered how Oliver would be the following day. He'd arranged a lunch with some donors, and now Alex waited for him to either call and cancel or to maybe apologize for the way he'd behaved. By noon, neither option had happened. The lunch was scheduled for one p.m. at the Hyatt. He showered and changed from his running gear into something casual but smart, a pair of light gray pants, a white button down and a navy-blue sports coat.

The lobby at the Hyatt was busy, but Alex spotted Oliver talking with two business-looking types in Brooks Brothers' suits. Alex tamped down the slight, jittery feeling he experienced when Oliver looked his way then said something to the two men who turned to watch him approach.

"Alex!" Oliver beamed at him. "Glad you could make it. Come meet our two VIP donors."

VIP, really? The men smiled at Alex and extended their hands. "Alex, want you to meet Colin Hundersfeld and Jasper Morrows. Gentlemen, this is *the* Alexander Martin who took the city by storm last night."

Alex shook hands with the men, noting that it was obvious Oliver was pretending nothing untoward had happened between them. That was okay. He could go with that. If Oliver wanted to ignore it, or perhaps he'd even forgotten his inappropriate behavior, then that was probably best.

He shook hands with the men then followed Oliver along with their host into the dining room. As they sat at their table Oliver winked at him and gave him a sly smile. They were definitely going to talk about what had happened, later. If Oliver got the message that 'fuck off' meant just that, there wouldn't be a problem. From his side anyway.

Lunch was okay. The guys were personable and enthusiastic about his work, but Alex couldn't wait to get away and call Blake. He needed the sound of his voice like a junkie needed a hit. Friday couldn't come soon enough and the thought of Blake and him in bed together, naked and banging like bunnies on crack, was enough to bring a salacious smile to his lips and for his dick to grow long and hard in his briefs. He flinched when he locked eyes with Oliver who was staring at him, his mouth slightly open and a knowing expression all over his tan face.

Damn. It was as if Oliver had been able to read his mind. No matter how hard he tried, he couldn't stop the heat that flooded his cheeks. He wanted to excuse himself and head for the men's room, but he didn't dare stand up. The bulge behind his fly in those too revealing light gray slacks would be a dead giveaway to Oliver. Instead, he grabbed his glass of Chardonnay and took a too-long swig of the wine. When he put the glass down, choking slightly, all three men were staring at him with varying degrees of amusement and concern.

"I'm all right," he mumbled trying to smile. "Something must have gone down the wrong way." He didn't dare look at Oliver. That smug smile was almost certain to be firmly in place.

After lunch, and after the two donors had left, Alex told Oliver he was going up to his room. Oliver walked with him to the elevators in the lobby. "I've arranged a pre-opening tour for tomorrow afternoon at four," he said, his hand on Alex's shoulder. "Doreen will be here by then, so you should feel safer."

"I feel very safe, thank you." Alex moved so that Oliver's hand fell from his shoulder.

"I was just trying to be a friend, you know."

"Friends do not go around groping, Oliver. Or persisting when I told you I had a boyfriend. I'm not a prude, but I don't cheat."

"Chrissakes, Alex, it would've been just foolin' around. I wasn't asking for a lifetime commitment."

"Thank God for that." Alex kept his voice level and his gaze fixed on Oliver's smug expression. "If you want to talk about last night, we can. It'll be brief. You tried to put a move on me, I told you to fuck off when you wouldn't take no for an answer. I hope that's an end to it. I really don't want to be looking over my shoulder every two minutes wondering where you are or what's on your mind."

Oliver smirked. "You need to get over yourself, Alexander Martin. You're not all that appealing."

"Oh, fine. Now we're into insults. I won't reciprocate although I have a few that come to mind. Just do your job, Oliver, and I'll do mine, and that way we'll get through the month ahead without any drama. Okay?"

The elevator door slid open, and Alex didn't wait for an answer from Oliver. The door closed on Oliver's sullen face, and Alex wondered if he'd want to break the contract and send Alex packing. It would be a huge inconvenience for him trying to find another exhibition to fill the suddenly empty space. Alex didn't think Oliver would go that far, but he was sure Doreen would get an earful when she arrived.

Oh, well.

* * * *

Blake read the latest text from Alex and frowned. It was obvious to Blake that Alex was playing down the situation between him and Oliver. Which was maybe the better way to handle it. He had to be there for a month, maybe longer if Oliver picked up the option for two more weeks. Honestly, he couldn't see why the creep wouldn't. Alex's work was terrific, and the gallery was bound to do a ton of business. Too bad the guy had turned out to be an ass. Doreen's arrival on Wednesday had no doubt eased matters, and he'd be there tomorrow night to do his best to make Alex feel a whole lot better.

He could not wait. He hadn't thought it possible to miss someone as much as he missed Alex. They hadn't been spending every night together, but enough that Blake was decidedly lonesome when he woke up without Alex's warm body next to him in bed. And it wasn't just the sex he was missing. He loved having Alex's company, loved hearing him laugh, loved…

"Oh hey, Blake." Roger Benson appeared at his office doorway. "Any news on the Herriot case?"

"I've requested a civil harassment restraining order from the court and attached the police report. Haven't heard anything yet."

"I guess if that works, we can forego pressing charges on the idiot. Are you okay with that? It's you he tried to hit with his nose."

"Every time you say that, it makes me laugh. Yeah, I'm fine with it. He's more trouble to himself really. Dale called yesterday and said they haven't seen or heard from him since his wife left."

"That's something, I guess. Well, keep me informed if anything changes. Oh, this is for you." He placed a file on Blake's desk. "Any questions, ask me."

"Will do." Blake admired Roger's ability to keep his emotions separate from his cases. Blake tended to get involved, perhaps a little too much, he thought. Joey's future happiness, for instance. He couldn't help wondering how the little guy was faring in his new home. Maybe Keren would call with an update at some point. Until then he'd just have to wonder. He'd told himself it wasn't his place to interfere unless there was a problem. And that would seem unlikely. Keren had been gung-ho about her friends fostering Joey, and Blake had to admit it did sound ideal.

Sighing, he opened the file Roger had left on his desk. A new case awaited his attention.

* * * *

Alex and Doreen left the gallery together after a successful Friday night showing. "I expect you're anxious to get back to the hotel," Doreen said, with a gentle tap on his shoulder.

Alex glanced at his watch. "Yeah, Blake should be there by now. He texted when his plane arrived. He said he'd wait in the lobby for me."

"Why don't we have lunch tomorrow? I'd like to spend more time with him, now that it looks as if you and he are a couple."

"That sounds good. Anywhere you're particularly fond of?"

"Roberto's on Embarcadero is nice."

"Okay, we'll meet you there. Say at noon?"

"Perfect, and I won't bring Oliver. He has a lot of wallowing to do before he's allowed to socialize with us." Doreen's smile was tight before she allowed it to reach her eyes, then she hugged Alex. "Don't worry, darling boy. I won't allow him to sully your name or reputation."

"Thanks, Doreen." He kissed her cheek. "See you tomorrow." The Uber she'd ordered pulled up to the curb, and he opened the door for her. "Goodnight, Doreen."

He waved as the car pulled away then turned and almost speed walked the two-block distance between the gallery and his hotel. When he burst through the glass doors into the lobby, he spotted Blake, who immediately jumped to his feet from the couch he'd been waiting on.

They rushed into each other's arms, their embrace hot, their kiss long enough to raise eyebrows and temperatures if there had been anyone else in the lobby. They were alone apart from the young male receptionist who was busy talking on the phone.

"Let's go," Alex mumbled against Blake's lips. "Let's not waste any time."

"No argument from me." After a quick kiss, he picked up his overnight bag, grabbed Alex's arm and together they ran to the elevator. Once inside and behind closed doors, they were in each other's arms again, Blake peppering Alex's face with burning kisses. The elevator doors slid open on Alex's floor, followed by the sound of a throat being cleared that had them springing apart.

Two young men stood there, grinning at them. "You had to do that, Colin?" one of them asked. "I was enjoying the view. These guys know how to kiss."

"Sorry," Blake muttered, grabbing his bag and hustling Alex out of the elevator.

"No problem. Have fun!"

"Oh, we will," Alex crowed as they sped down the hallway. They were laughing so hard, Alex made a mess of getting the key card in the slot to unlock the door. "If you'd stop kissing my neck, maybe I could concentrate more on getting this damned door open."

"Success!" Blake yelled when at last the door opened, and they fell into the room. Blake threw his bag aside. "Nice place, but where's the bed? There's no bed?"

Still laughing, Alex pushed Blake farther into the room. "Stop panicking, the bed's on the other side of that screen. Come see." He took Blake's hand and dragged him behind the screen. "See? A bed."

"Oh wow, king-size. We have to get one of these when—"

Alex nuzzled Blake's neck. "When what, sweetheart?"

"When...uh, you know, when we..."

"Keep going," Alex murmured. He slid a hand down the front of Blake's pants, then massaged his erection, all the while kissing his jaw, his throat, and loving the whimpers that broke free from Blake's lips.

"I-I can't think when you do that. You're melting my brain."

"Let's take a shower together," Alex said. "I know I need one after this long day, and it'll help clear your brain, right?"

"Right, shower. Good idea."

Alex smiled. "I love you so much." He unbuttoned Blake's shirt, pausing to lick at the nipples he exposed on the hard pecs before easing the shirt over Blake's broad shoulders. "Mmm..." Alex leered at Blake's bare chest with its dusting of dark hair. "You are one delicious man. I want to lick you all over."

"Let's shower first." Blake tugged Alex's polo over his head. "I'll taste better."

"Matter of opinion," Alex muttered, but followed Blake into the bathroom where they discarded the rest of their clothes. Blake turned on the water, and they stepped under the warm spray, holding each other in a tight embrace while the water cascaded over them.

Blake slipped behind Alex and reached for the soap. He began soaping Alex's back, his fingers massaging and caressing the length of his spine.

"Mmm, that feels good." Alex wriggled his butt into Blake's groin, relishing the feel of Blake's erection that nestled between his ass cheeks. He let his head fall back onto Blake's shoulder and shivered with delight when Blake traced a trail of kisses over his throat up to his lips. Alex turned his head so that they could kiss less awkwardly, and their tongues could slide together. Blake pushed a soapy finger into the cleft between Alex's buttocks, probing then penetrating his tight hole.

Alex let out a long, breathy sigh and bore down on Blake's finger, taking him all the way inside. Blake encircled Alex's body with one arm, holding him steady while he covered his neck and shoulders with hot, searing kisses. Alex writhed against him, moaning softly when Blake grasped his erection and pumped it with slow, rhythmic strokes.

Blake dropped to his knees behind Alex, replacing his finger with his tongue, burrowing deep inside him. Alex groaned, his body arching in ecstasy as he leaned back, moving his ass in slow circles around Blake's thrusting tongue. Alex, drunk with desire, tried to tamp down the orgasm building inside him. It was too soon. He loved this, wanted this, but he wanted all of

Blake inside him — every inch of that beautiful hard cock. As if he had intuited Alex's need, Blake got to his feet, sliding his tongue up the length of Alex's spine. He tightened his arms around his lover's lean-muscled torso.

"Oh, yeah." Alex wriggled in Blake's arms. "Got a feeling your dick's getting impatient."

Blake's deep voice vibrated on Alex's ear. "It wants in."

"It's not the only one." Alex shut off the water and slid the shower door open. He stepped out, grabbed a towel and handed it to Blake who wrapped it around them both, going for a quicker drying session.

"Good enough." He threw the towel to one side and practically shoved Alex out of the bathroom.

"Eager much?" Alex was laughing when Blake tossed him onto the bed then dived on top of him.

"You have no idea. Five days without you is five days way too many." Blake yelped with surprise when Alex rolled him onto his back and covered his chest with kisses.

"The feeling is entirely mutual," Alex mumbled between kisses. He lingered over both nipples, licking them, teasing them with his teeth. He kissed his way over Blake's hard torso to his cock, taking the head between his lips, then sliding down its length with one long, gliding movement that had Blake writhing under him, moaning with ecstasy.

Alex scraped at the base of Blake's erection with his teeth, nibbling gently at the hard flesh. He backed up little by little, swirling his tongue around the hot, rigid length until he reached the head. Gripping Blake's cock in his fist, he gulped at the pre-cum oozing from the slit, savoring the sweet and salty taste.

"Oh, my God," Blake panted. "You get better at that all the time."

Alex grinned up at him. "Practice makes perfect, they say."

"Ride me." Blake slid his hands onto Alex's hips and pulled him up so that he sat astride Blake's thighs. Alex reached for the lube set on the nightstand and readied himself for Blake's cock. He raised up slightly and pushed his lubed fingers into his hole, undulating his pelvis as he took one then two of his fingers inside himself.

Blake stared up at him through glazed, lust-filled eyes. "God, but you are so beautiful, and a turn-on like nothing I've ever seen."

"You should see what I can right now. Michelangelo would've gone mad over that chest of yours. Remind me to have my camera ready the next time I'm straddling you like this."

He guided the head of his lover's throbbing erection into the cleft between his buttocks then eased himself down onto the hard shaft. His breath hissed through his teeth when the rigid flesh slid inside him, the burn bearable, knowing it would give way to the ultimate pleasure ahead. They locked eyes, and their bodies began to rock together, slowly at first then, as passion and overwhelming sensation took over, with a fervor that had them both moaning out loud.

"Oh my God, yes, Blake. Feels wonderful. Fuck me hard so I can feel you inside me after you've gone back to LA."

Blake thrust upward again and again, pounding into Alex's ass relentlessly. Alex groaned and leaned back, supporting himself with his hands flat on the mattress on either side of him while he moved to his own rhythm up and down on the hard length of Blake's cock. His eyes rolled back, and he gave himself up to the exquisite rapture that surged through him, the pressure on his prostate from each stroke of Blake's cock like tiny electric jolts of pleasure that made him see stars.

Alex gasped when Blake took his erection in a firm grip, and the first warning signs of his impending orgasm rippled through his spine and groin into his balls. The sensation was too good to resist, and even though he wanted this to last forever, he couldn't overcome the need to thrust even harder through Blake's fist. The wrenching cry that was torn from him became a joyful shout as he came, splattering cum all over Blake's chest and face.

Blake grasped Alex's hips and rammed into him hard and fast. His body stiffened and he gasped out Alex's name as he climaxed. He reared up and drew Alex into his arms. Alex clung to him, clenching his ass muscles around the base of Blake's cock, reliving the sensation of the hot surge of Blake's cum inside him over and over again. A sensation like no other, one he wanted to experience again and again.

He peppered Blake's jaw and throat with kisses. The two of them were laughing and crying and rambling incoherently until Blake fell back on the mattress, taking Alex with him, holding him pressed tight against him, his lips on Alex's in a tender kiss that quietened them both and let them sink into the bliss of sweet euphoria.

Chapter Sixteen

They dozed then woke to make love again then showered, and only hunger pangs made them delay their third go-around. Blake admitted he hadn't eaten all day. Alex had met Doreen for lunch, but that seemed like a long time ago.

"I better order some room service before we die from lack of nutrition or something," Alex suggested as they dried each other.

"They'll serve us at this time of night?" Blake looked skeptical.

"Twenty-four seven it says on the menu. I'll check it out. Sandwich or pizza or should we have breakfast? It is almost five o'clock."

"That sounds good. How about eggs benedict?"

"That does sound good." He slipped on the white robe the hotel supplied then picked up the phone and placed the order, adding coffee and orange juice. "Twenty minutes," he told Blake after hanging up. "What on earth can we do to fill twenty minutes?"

"Watch TV?"

"Try again."

"Read a book?"

"Funny guy."

Blake pulled him into his arms. "Make out?"

"Now you're talkin'." He opened his robe and pressed his naked body to Blake's—Blake hadn't bothered with a robe. "Mmm, feels so fine. Time for a quickie?"

"Don't like quickies. I like to savor every part of you, nice and slow." He licked Alex's throat, lingering over his Adam's apple, sucking on it gently.

"Now you have me harder than a baseball bat, so you have to get me off before room service gets here."

"Bossy boy," Blake murmured, dropping to his knees. "Bossy boy with a beautiful dick." He held it in his hand and pressed his lips to the crease between Alex's thigh and groin. Alex's legs trembled when Blake moved to kiss his way under Alex's balls, using his tongue to trace and lick his taint, pushing in far enough to reach his hole.

"Blake..." Alex gasped and carded his fingers through Blake's curly hair.

Blake looked up at him from under his thick, dark eyelashes and smiled. He gripped Alex's erection at its base then ran his tongue up the hot length before devouring and taking it all the way to the back of his throat. He slid his lips up and down over the hard, throbbing length while he stroked and teased Alex's balls, bringing muffled groans of pleasure from him. Blake caressed Alex's butt, squeezing the twin globes of smooth, round flesh. He slipped a finger into the cleft and probed at Alex's opening and heard his breath catch in his throat as Blake slid his finger inside him.

His cock pulsed in Blake's mouth and pre-cum spilled over his tongue when he found and stroked Alex's sweet spot. Blake could tell Alex was close and he sucked harder, urging Alex on. He cupped Alex's ass cheeks and pulled him deeper into his mouth. Alex's body stiffened and he groaned, and Blake gulped and swallowed the torrent of hot salty cream that filled his mouth. He threw his arms around Alex's waist, holding him until the spasms subsided.

Blake relaxed his hold on Alex enough so that he could sink to his knees then he gathered him close and pressed a long, hard kiss to his lips.

"You are amazing," Alex panted, sliding a hand down Blake's torso to capture his erection. "Now, your turn."

A knock on the door and a voice singing out, "Room service!" had them both springing to their feet. Laughing, Blake ran for the bathroom. "You have the robe on, you get the door."

"Son of a gun," Alex muttered, hastily fastening his robe tie around himself. He swung the door opened and was greeted with a young waiter's bright smile.

"Good morning, sir. Getting an early start to the day?" he asked, pushing the trolley in front of him into the room.

"Yes, something like that." He wasn't about to explain the real reason for the early call.

"So, eggs benedict for two, with a side of hash browns, whole wheat toast with preserves, orange juice and a pot of coffee. Anything else I can get you in addition, sir?"

"No, that's great, thank you." He handed the waiter a tip and opened the door for him. "Thanks again."

"You're welcome, sir."

Alex knocked on the bathroom door. "You can come out now, chicken."

The door flew open, and a still naked Blake grabbed him. "Who're you calling chicken?" Any more taunting from Alex was silenced when Blake's mouth crashed against his. He was lifted off his feet and carried across the room before being tossed onto the bed.

"Wow, having sex all night sure agrees with you," Alex teased when Blake freed his lips.

"And we're going to have more right up until you have to leave for the afternoon gallery tour." Blake rolled him onto his side and attacked his nipples.

"The eggs'll get cold." Alex laughed. "I can't believe I said that."

"Nor can I, but you're right. We need to eat to keep up our energy levels." He sat up and reached for his robe. "What time d'you have to be at the gallery?"

"Oh, I forgot to mention we're meeting Doreen for lunch at the Embarcadero, first. The tour's not until two."

"Darn. Lunch with Doreen instead of sex with you. How will I survive?"

"I'll make it up to you later tonight."

"You bet you will."

Alex grabbed his hand and led him over to the table where their breakfast was set. "And we 're not meeting Doreen until noon, so there's time before then."

Blake patted Alex's ass. "You say all the best things."

* * * *

Lunch with Doreen was fun, and Blake decided he liked her a lot. It was obvious she thought the world of Alex, and he couldn't fault her for that. Things took a decided downturn when they entered the gallery. Oliver glared at the three of them as they entered.

"You've had lunch, I presume?"

Doreen nodded and smiled. "Yes, I wanted to get to know Blake a little better and it seemed a pleasant way of doing just that."

Oliver fixed Blake with a hostile stare, and Alex took a step forward. "Oliver, this is my boyfriend, Blake Carson. We would have asked you to join us for lunch, but you said you had some business calls to make."

Some instinct told Blake not to offer his hand for the man to shake. He knew it would be ignored, and Oliver would preen to himself that he had snubbed Alex's *boyfriend*.

What a douche.

"I did have a lot of business calls to make." Oliver made no effort to ease the tension he'd created. "And I still have others to take care of." He turned on his heel and strode toward a door Blake presumed was to his office.

"Well..." Blake rolled his eyes. "He sure as hell won't win any accolades for host of the week."

Doreen sighed. "He's the original drama queen, and if you ask me, royally pissed that Alex has you in his life. Alex told me he tried to put the make on him the very first night Alex was here, and I have told him to act like a professional and leave the talent alone."

Alex laughed but Blake could tell he was uncomfortable. He took Alex's hand in a gentle grip. "Well, I won't hang around just to put his nose out of joint and make things difficult for either of you, so I'll see you back at the hotel, Alex."

"But you will come tonight, won't you?" Alex held on to his hand. "It's the official opening. I know it feels as if we've already had an opening night, but this is the one Oliver advertised for the general public along with his cronies."

"Yes, I'll be here, don't worry. I can disappear amongst the throng of your admirers so that Oliver doesn't get irritated by my presence."

"He's being an ass," Doreen said. "And I'll be here to keep you company should you need me."

Blake smiled at her. "Thanks, Doreen." He leaned in to kiss Alex on the cheek. "See you later, honey." *Hope that asshole's watching.* Alex looked downcast so Blake wrapped him up in a hug. "It's just a couple of hours, and I'll be waiting for you."

"I know." Alex sighed. "I'm being silly. I didn't realize just how much of a prick Oliver is. He couldn't even say hi to you. What a jerk."

"That he is." Blake stepped back from their hug. "Okay, see you later. Have a good tour."

His cell chimed as he left the gallery. Glancing at the screen, he frowned. "Hi, Dale, what's up?"

"That idiot Fred Herriot is outside our door calling us all kinds of names and yelling that he's gonna sue us for harassment. Can you believe him? I want to go punch him on the nose, but Henry won't let me open the door."

"Call the local precinct, Dale. They already have him on report, and he's breaking the restraining order restrictions. Call me back and let me know what action the cops take. I'm in San Francisco right now but I'll be back Sunday night. Don't confront the man—he's borderline nuts."

"Okay, I'll call the cops." He hung up, and Blake cursed under his breath. That fool was going to end up in jail if he kept this up.

When he got back to the hotel, the maid was in the room, so he went back to the lobby to wait for Dale's call. He couldn't help wondering how on earth Alex was going to deal with another three weeks of Oliver Stevenson. He worried, that out of spite, he might talk negatively about Alex's work. The man was a moron, but was he stupid enough to sabotage his own gallery's exhibition just because he couldn't get in Alex's pants? He hoped that wasn't the case, but it hadn't taken Blake long to realize there was something slimy about Stevenson.

His cell chimed, and he gave Dale his full attention. "What's the news, Dale?"

"The cops took their time getting here, but they warned Fred he was in violation of a restraining order." Dale laughed. "He told them to go fuck themselves, not just once or twice but over and over until they cuffed him and dragged his ass out of here. It was quite the scene. The neighbors just couldn't believe it. It's like he's lost his mind. I don't know where it's going from here."

"They'll most likely have him face a judge for the restraining order violation, but that won't be until Monday, if even that soon. I'll be back in town, so I'll show up at the hearing once I clarify the date and time. From the way he's behaving, I won't be surprised if he mouths off at the judge. Until then, though, you don't have to worry. They can keep him locked up until the court date."

"That's good, I guess. We're hoping he'll sell and we'll finally be done with him."

"We can but hope," Blake said. "But he'll have to toe the line while he's living in your building, or he'll end up being arrested more times than he can count."

* * * *

When Alex arrived at their hotel room, he looked tired and strained. Blake took him in his arms and pressed a soothing kiss to his cheek. "Oliver still being an asshole?"

"He and Doreen had a blazing row, and she threatened to pull my work from his gallery if he didn't grow up. As it is, she said she'd spread the word about him being difficult to work with. Not that it's a big deal. So many in the industry are difficult to work with, but he didn't like her telling him he's acting like a child."

"Will she be there tonight?"

"Oh yeah." He sagged in Blake's arms. "I am so wiped out. I guess the lack of sleep caught up with me. Wouldn't want to have missed out on anything though," he added, kissing Blake's neck.

"Plus you had a stressful day thanks to moron number one. Come on..." He led Alex over to the bed. "You need a nap." He started to undress Alex, who stood there, his head on Blake's shoulder and let him do it. Blake lowered him onto the bed and tucked him in.

"You have to get in here with me," Alex whined.

Blake chuckled. "Okay, but no getting frisky. You need to sleep."

"Don't think I have any frisky in me." He yawned. "But I want you here beside me."

"Okay." Blake shucked off his shirt, shoes and pants and climbed in next to Alex. By the time he lay down, Alex was snoring softly. Blake watched him sleep for a while until he too started to drift. He spooned Alex from behind, his lips on Alex's nape, and slept.

* * * *

Alex stared at his mother and father in complete shock. "You're sending me where?"

"Somewhere they know how to deal with sinners like you," his father said, sneering at him.

He looked at his mother, tears brimming in his eyes. "You think I'm a sinner? I haven't done anything wrong, Mom."

"You were seen with that Carson boy in the woods," she snapped. "Such vile behavior is forbidden by the Lord. You know that. You've heard it in church and you've heard us say it time and time again. The Lord must be obeyed."

"And we're sending you to those who can set you on a path to righteousness," his father added. "It's a good place, better than you deserve, and when you're cured you can come home."

"Cured? But I'm not sick."

His father grunted. "Only a sick person would do what you were seen doing with the Carson boy, or any other boy for that matter. You are sick, Alex, and you must be cured if you are to remain our son."

Alex felt his legs shake. They were serious. They were going to send him away. Away from home. Away from Blake. "No, you can't!" He turned and ran to the door, wrenched it open and barreled straight into a tall man's broad chest. The man held him by the arms, his strength unmistakable.

"So, this is him?" the man asked, and his father replied with another grunt.

"His mother has packed a suitcase with the basics as you instructed. Take him."

Alex screamed, but the man clamped a hand over his mouth and hustled him into a black SUV where another man was waiting to hold him down. His suitcase was thrown in beside them, and the vehicle pulled away from his home.

"No, no, no!"

"Alex!" He fought the arms around him that held him pressed to a hard chest. "Alex, it's all right. You were dreaming. It's Blake. You're safe, sweetheart, you're safe."

"Blake," he whispered. "*Blake*, oh my God." He turned in his lover's arms and anchored himself to the strong body he adored. "I haven't had that dream in so long. I thought I was over those memories. I'm sorry. Did I scare you?"

"No, you didn't scare me. I was scared for you. You want to talk about it?"

For a long moment it seemed as if Alex were going to shake his head or say no, but then... "I used to have that dream a lot after they sent me to Farmton. My folks telling me they were sending me away to be cured, and all I could think of was that I wouldn't see *you* anymore. I tried to run, but they had this bruiser there to stop me. He threw me in the back seat of a black van. There was another man there to make sure I didn't bolt. I fought him but he was twice my size. I remember trying to open the door, looking out the window yelling for my mom and dad, and they just stood there, watching the van pull away.

"I'm not ashamed to admit I cried, but it was more tears of rage. I just couldn't believe they'd do this to me. Throw me away like I was nothing to them. Then, as the days and weeks went by and they never came for me, I knew they didn't care, didn't want me in their lives anymore, and I grew to hate them more and more each day."

"Jesus." Blake held him tighter and kissed his forehead. "Sweetheart, I am so sorry I wasn't there to help you through that."

"You didn't know where they'd sent me."

"If only I'd thought to ask your Aunt Katherine."

"And then what? You were a kid like me. The guys they had there all seemed like they were seven feet tall, and they were mean." He shivered. "I'm glad you didn't know. They might have hurt you." He was quiet for a while, thinking. "I guess that letter from my dad's attorney brought it all to the fore in my mind. And that row Doreen had with Oliver had me stressed out. I think I want to go home, Blake. Screw all this. It's not worth it."

"Yes, it is." Blake framed his face with the palms of his hands. "You are not giving up on this exhibition. It's what you worked for, strived for. It's your talent that got you here, not a prick like Oliver Stevenson. Don't let him diminish that...or you."

Alex sighed. "You're right of course. To walk away would be admitting defeat, that he got to me, and I ran home crying like a baby."

"And you're not a baby." Blake kissed him. "You're a strong, brave man. Not many could've survived what you've been through. I love you."

"Love you too. You're so good for me." Alex returned the kiss. "You're everything that's been missing in my life, and now I've got you, I don't ever want to lose you again."

"No chance of that, ever." He grinned. "Remember I sang *Stuck Like Glue* to you. Want a repeat performance?"

"Not your singing, maybe, but I know something I want a repeat performance of. Repeat and repeat till we both drop."

"Easily done, my boy." He rolled Alex onto his back. "Ready for me?"

"Always."

Chapter Seventeen

They were late getting to the gallery. Not a lot, just a few minutes, but enough to have Oliver glaring at them when they entered. He strode over to them, grabbed Alex by the arm and yanked him away from Blake.

"I have my people waiting to meet you!" he all but snarled. "Where have you been?"

Alex wrenched his arm from the man's grasp, his shoulders hunched as if he were about to throw a left hook.

Blake stepped in front of him. Keeping his voice low, he said, "If you don't want a scene in front of your *people*, I suggest you calm the fuck down. Don't play grabby-hands with my boyfriend or I will put you on your ass. Where we have been is none of your business, but Alex is here now, and you will play your part of the congenial and professional gallery owner you're supposed to be. Okay?"

A few seconds ticked by, and it seemed that Oliver would self-implode, then, as if someone had turned a switch in his brain, his expression morphed from malicious to benign, and he nodded.

"Of course, what was I thinking? Alex, would you mind accompanying me over to meet some friends of mine?"

Alex's shoulders visibly relaxed. "Not at all. Lead the way."

Blake watched the two men walk across the gallery floor to where a small group of men and women waited. Doreen was suddenly at his side.

"I have to commend you on your handling of that ridiculous man," she said.

"He's lucky I didn't want Alex's night ruined. Any other time and I'd have laid him out. I've dealt with people like him in law courts, all bluster and ego, typical bully. Call them out, and they fold."

"Still, it was great how you kept it so low-key. Nobody really noticed what was going on, except those two young guys over there. But I think they were more interested in scoping you and Alex out rather than what you were saying to the man-child."

"I like you, Doreen," Blake said. "You're good for Alex. You won't let guys like Oliver take advantage of his good nature."

"And you're good for him too, in a way I could never be." She patted his arm. "Let's go get a drink. They're free."

"The best kind." He gave her his arm, and they strolled over to the bar. After he'd ordered a gin and tonic for Doreen and a Scotch on the rocks for himself, he positioned himself so he could watch the interaction between Alex, Oliver and the group of Oliver's people.

"I wouldn't worry too much about Alex," Doreen said. "He's a tough cookie when it comes to his work.

Then again, after what he's been through in his life, he's had to be. You don't go through the school of hard knocks without learning how to defend yourself."

Blake nodded. "I had no idea what had happened to him when he disappeared from my life. His parents wouldn't give me any information, and now of course, I know why. He said he came looking for me when he got out of Farmton, but we'd moved by then. It was a miracle that I was passing your gallery that day, and you more or less coerced me into going inside. You have my everlasting gratitude for that."

Doreen smiled. "One of my better moves. In the back of my crazy old mind, I thought, he's so good-looking — I bet he's Alex's type."

"Did you really?" Blake laughed then leaned down to kiss her cheek. "Thank you again."

"If I believed in miracles, I'd say you were heaven sent that day."

"I'll drink to that." He held his glass up to hers, and they clinked them together.

"By the way, Alex told me you were thinking of fostering some abused kid. How's that going?"

"I had to give up on that. Keren, the woman from social services I met in court at the hearing against Joey's foster parents, found him a home. A good home with friends of hers. So, although I was disappointed, in a way it worked out for the best."

"I can tell from that wry tone in your voice that you're not completely over the disappointment."

Blake sighed. "You caught me, but it really is the best outcome for Joey. More than anything, he needs a home where he feels safe and loved, after what he's been through."

"And he would've gotten that from you, without a doubt. And I'm guessing Alex, down the road. He told me he's asked you to move in with him."

"We're talking about it. I keep thinking it's too soon. Just about a month, although Alex keeps adding the twenty years to it." He smiled. "He's pretty keen on the idea."

Doreen nodded. "It's a big step, but just so you know, I think you guys are the perfect couple. The way you look at each other? Wow. I don't remember any of my beaus looking at me like that. Even the two I married. Oh, oh, look out. Here comes trouble." She frowned at Oliver, who was approaching them at a fast pace.

Too fast, Blake thought, *like he's on speed or something.* As he drew close, Blake could see his pupils were dilated. *For sure on something.*

"You might be interested to know that while you two were over here having way too much fun, Alex sold two of his prints. One of you..." He gave Blake a sarcastic smile. "At the swimming hole."

Doreen giggled. "Yeah, I can guarantee that perky ass is on many a living room wall across the nation."

Blake's face grew hot. "Really? I never even thought about that."

Oliver stared at him then shook his head. "Well, to each his own, I guess," he muttered before striding away.

"What did that mean?"

"It was meant to be a put-down, of course," Doreen told him. "Oliver's pissed that he can't woo Alex away from you, and he thinks he's a much better catch than you. He's so jealous his skin is turning green."

"It's gonna be puce if he tries to get between Alex and me, again."

"That's my boy." Doreen ordered another round of drinks. "But I don't think you'll ever have to worry about that. Alex is so in love with you, no other being exists in his world."

Blake smiled. "Good to know."

At the end of the evening Oliver wanted them to stay behind and have a drink with him, but Doreen shot that idea down with a few choice words.

"You've already had too much to drink, Olly, and you know how you behave when you're in your cups. I'll call an Uber for you. No way you'll drive home tonight."

At first, Blake thought Oliver was going to give in to Doreen taking charge, but just as earlier, when his expression had changed from sneering malice to contrition, now his outrage was stamped all over his face.

"Don't tell me what I can and cannot do in my own gallery, Doreen! Fucking bitch. This is the last time I want to see you in here."

"Oliver, I represent Alexander Martin, and I will be where he needs me," Doreen snapped. "Especially when he has to deal with a predatory snake like you."

"Why you —!" He raised his hand as if to strike her, and Blake moved in to grab his arm.

"Whoa! You need to calm down, mister, and don't even dare try what you were about to." He pulled Oliver away from Doreen then pushed him onto a nearby bench where he seemed to sag into himself, a dazed expression replacing the previous anger.

"Sorry," he mumbled. "Sorry, Doreen, Alex. I'm drunk, but that's no excuse." He looked up at Blake through bloodshot eyes. "You must think I'm a total asshole." He tried to stand but fell back on the bench.

Blake helped him up. "I think Doreen's suggestion of an Uber is a good one."

Oliver nodded, and Doreen fished her cell out of her bag and punched in a number. "Five minutes. Let's get you outside into the fresh air, Olly. You'll feel better."

Meekly, Oliver allowed Doreen and Blake to guide him out of the gallery. He handed Alex his keys to lock up. "Keep them for the Sunday afternoon showing. I might do you all a favor and take some time off."

"Are you sure?" Alex gazed at him with concern. "I'll call you tomorrow to make sure you're okay."

They all sighed with relief when the Uber showed up and Oliver was seated in the back. Doreen spoke to the driver. "Make sure he gets into the lobby of his building. The doorman on duty will take care of him from there." She stepped back and watched the car pull away. "He really needs to go into rehab," she said, with a trace of sadness.

"You think he will?" Alex asked.

"I'll try my best to convince him. He's not such an arrogant jerk when he's sober, but he also has a cocaine habit, and it doesn't mix well with booze."

"Yeah, I could tell he was on something when we first arrived," Blake said. "His aggression was a sure sign he was high."

Doreen sighed. "Anyway, you boys go and have fun. When do you leave, Blake?"

"Unfortunately, late tomorrow afternoon. I would stay longer but I've got a case I have to stay on top of. I'll see you before I go."

Of course." She leaned in to kiss his cheek then Alex's. "Ah, my chariot arrives." She waved at the Uber driver. "Goodnight, you handsome devils. See you tomorrow."

"Goodnight," they chorused, then hand-in-hand, they walked back to the hotel.

* * * *

"Blake?" Roger Benson stood in his office doorway one week later. "You busy?"

"Not really. Just finished the Herriot-Bloomfield case, so if you have something else for me, I'm available."

Roger entered and sat opposite Blake. "Another abuse case, I'm afraid. The hearing is on Monday at nine a.m. The husband's accused by both his wife and underage daughter. Here's the file. You can look at it over the weekend. Do you have plans?"

Blake nodded. "I'm flying to San Francisco tonight, but I'll be back Sunday."

"Well, you have a good time. I'll see you on Monday. Safe travels."

"Thanks, Roger." It had been a strange week, starting with the confrontation between Oliver, Alex, Doreen and himself. He'd gone with Alex to the gallery Sunday afternoon, and Oliver had been a no-show. It was just as well that he'd given Alex a set of keys. There had been people already lining up outside the gallery. Blake had been sorry to leave later that day, but Alex had everything under control like he knew he would, and Doreen had been there to help him answer questions from interested patrons.

When he and Alex had spoken that night, Alex had told him Oliver had called, said he was okay and he'd be coming to the gallery midweek for the PR meeting he'd arranged ahead of time. They'd talked every night, texted each other several times a day and it had helped ease the loneliness they both admitted to, but Blake couldn't wait until Alex was back in Los Angeles.

On the home front, the case he was handling for Dale and Henry Bloomfield had ended with Fred Herriot going berserk in the cell he shared with two other men. He'd punched one of his cell mates and a police officer and, as Blake had predicted, thrown a fit in court. He'd been sent for psychological evaluation, and in the meantime a sworn statement from his wife accusing him of abuse had been entered into evidence against him. He'd be gone for a couple of years at least.

Poor Fred...not. At least Dale and Henry could enjoy their home in peace. He'd spoken with them earlier, and they'd said to celebrate they were going to throw the housewarming party they'd put off indefinitely because of Fred.

"And you must come, Blake," Dale had insisted. *"Thanks to you we can start having our parents and friends over. We never dared before in case Fred started rampaging all over the place."*

"Okay if I bring a friend?"

"Of course. Boyfriend?"

"Yes. A guy I knew when I was a kid. His name is Alex. We just happened to reconnect about five weeks ago. Kind of like a miracle, really."

"How romantic. We'll look forward to meeting him. Thanks, Blake for everything you did for us."

"My pleasure. Enjoy your home and tell Henry I said hi."

"Will do, and I'll be in touch with the date for the party. Bye."

"Bye, Dale."

He sat back in his chair and smiled, realizing he'd referred to their reunion as 'a kind of miracle' twice now. Once, while speaking with Doreen, and this time with Dale. But it was a miracle in a way. He didn't quite believe in such things, but the chances of him and Alex meeting again were millions to one. They hadn't managed to connect in Charlottesville, a much smaller city compared to Los Angeles, and yet somehow it had happened, and whether a miracle, or fate, or whatever, he was just happy it had.

And thank you, Doreen, for giving me that extra push.

* * * *

Alex was still a little wary around Oliver. He had apologized for being an ass, and the PR meeting had gone very well, but every now and then Alex would be aware of Oliver's eyes on him. Long, steady stares that made him uncomfortable.

Maybe he's not as sorry as he said, or that he should be. A guy like Oliver doesn't shed his arrogance overnight.

It was obvious he was used to getting his own way, in business and in his personal life. After the PR meeting, Oliver introduced Alex to Dominic Farrar, an artist, a nervous young man with a pretty face and slight build. Oliver pulled out his phone and showed Alex some of Dominic's work.

"I think Dominic's ready for his first exhibition, and I am honored that he has agreed it be at my gallery."

"Congratulations, Dominic," Alex said, shaking the young man's slightly damp hand. "I'm sure it will be a great success."

Later, Alex prepared to leave the gallery. Oliver and Dominic had ensconced themselves in Oliver's office with the blinds drawn. Alex paused on his way to the exit. *What was that noise?* After listening for a few seconds he was sure it could only be caused by the two men having sex. *They must have thought I'd left.*

Oliver's cries of "Oh yeah, Dom, that's it, right there, deeper, faster," took Alex by surprise.

So, fey Dominic was a top and Mr. Magnificent...wasn't. At least not in this scenario. Alex knew he shouldn't stereotype, but there was something pretty damn hilarious about what he was listening to. Groans and howls ensued, and Alex figured he'd better beat a hasty retreat before the laughter he was trying like mad to hold inside slipped out.

"Oh my God, Dom. I want that fucking great big prick of yours up my ass every day from now on!"

No reply from the owner of said prick, but it was, without a doubt, time for Alex to go.

Well, looks like I don't have to worry about Oliver trying to get in my pants anymore. Sounds like he's met his perfect man. Who knew?

Alex left the gallery thankful that he wouldn't have to face Oliver until the following evening. Once he got back to his hotel room, he poured himself a glass of wine then sat on the couch so he could call Blake and give him the latest news.

"Hi, honey. You have time to talk?"

"For you, of course. I just got home. How's it going?"

"Great, but I have some news."

"You sound okay," Blake said. "So it can't be bad news, can it?"

"It's *interesting*. So, I'm walking back to the hotel from the gallery, and I get a text from Oliver telling me he's not going to pick up the two-week option at the end of the month. Can't say I'm broken-hearted."

"Did he give a reason?" Blake asked.

"No, but I already know what it is."

"And?"

"A new interest. A young artist, aptly named Dominic."

"Why aptly named?"

"Are you sitting down?"

"Yes, having a glass of wine."

"Good, me too. Oliver introduced me to Dominic Farrar this afternoon. He does watercolors. Beautiful actually."

"The watercolors or the artist?"

"Both. He's very pretty, very young, and Oliver is putting on an exhibition for him after mine is over. However, it was the exhibition Oliver was putting on for Dominic in his office that caught my attention."

"Oh, yeah?"

"Yeah. I couldn't see what was going on, but I could sure as hell hear it and from the sounds of it, *Dom* was giving Oliver the fucking of his life. He had Oliver howling—literally."

"Oh, my God!"

"I know." They were both laughing like fools, and Alex told himself he shouldn't. "We shouldn't laugh, should we?" he choked out.

"Yes, we should. That is priceless. Hence, Dom's name being apt."

"Right. The little guy was in total control. Don't think we have to worry about Oliver showing any interest in yours truly anymore."

"That's a relief. How was the PR thingy?"

"Good. I will say Oliver knows what he's doing when it comes to promoting. Anyway, how are you?"

"Missing you. Can't wait till Friday to see you, kiss you, make love to you."

Alex groaned. "Are you naked?"

"Boxer briefs still on." Blake chuckled. "Phone sex?"

"Please. I know I'll see you on Friday, but it feels like it's still a long way off." They'd indulged quite a few times in the last couple of weeks, and although it was no way close to being hot, like the real thing, it did seem that both their imaginations were fine-tuned enough to at least take the edge off their longing for each other. It was the kissing that Alex missed. They'd tried making kissy noises but all that had done was reduce them to hysterics. He was giggling now.

"You're gonna ruin the mood if you start laughing," Blake said.

"Sorry, I was thinking of the night we tried to kiss over the phone."

"Oh my God, blank that from your mind right now. Shit, now I'm laughing."

Alex made a gross sucking noise into his phone. "Turning you on?"

"No! Okay settle down. Imagine me lying over you, stroking your cock, licking your nipples…"

"Okay, got it now. I'm hard already."

"You're so easy."

"Lucky you."

"Yeah." Alex could hear the smile in Blake's voice. "Lucky me."

Chapter Eighteen

In a repeat of the previous Friday evening, Blake jumped to his feet from the couch in the hotel lobby as Alex came barreling through the revolving door and straight into Blake's arms. This time, there were several people along with Blake in the lobby and the chorus of wolf-whistles and shouts of "Get a room" had them jumping apart, red-faced, and racing hand-in-hand for the elevator.

In the room, clothes were discarded at record-breaking speed, and they fell onto the bed with legs and arms wrapped around each other, lips and tongues meshed in searing kisses. All thoughts of overcrowded airports and jampacked planes fled from Blake's mind as Alex plundered his mouth with his brain-melting kisses, grinding his erection, slippery with pre-cum, against Blake's, bringing him way too fast to the edge.

"Wait, wait," he gasped. "You're gonna make me come too fast."

Alex gave him an evil grin. "That's okay. There's plenty more where that *comes* from."

Blake groaned. "Jokes, really? C'mere." He rolled Alex onto his back, covering his chest and abs with hot, sucking kisses. Alex arched his body into Blake's, writhing under him, while Blake inched closer to Alex's throbbing erection. He ran his tongue over the hot rock-hard flesh then up and down the length, coasting over and under Alex's balls, then back up to the tip before he swallowed him whole, straight down to the root.

He pulled back then lifted Alex's legs so he could bury his face deep between Alex's butt cheeks, circling his hole with the tip of his tongue. Alex bucked and writhed under him, panting out mumbled words like, "More...yeah, oh God, Blake, so good, so fucking good." Encouraged, Blake delved deeper, his tongue inside Alex's heat.

Alex whimpered, hands clutching at the sheet under him, bunching it as if in an effort to anchor himself to the euphoria Blake could tell from his blissed-out expression, overwhelmed him. "Blake, you have to fuck me," he rasped, sounding almost manic.

"I'm going to, don't worry," Blake said, lifting Alex's legs higher. He reached for the lube and thrust his slicked fingers into Alex's opening. Alex moaned, a dirty but deeply satisfied sound that had the effect of hardening Blake's cock to an almost painful degree. Without hesitating he pushed inside Alex who arched into the invasion, taking Blake all the way in and clenching his inner muscles around Blake's shaft to hold him there.

"Oh, yeah," Alex murmured, wriggling his ass. "Perfect." He wrapped an arm around Blake's neck and pressed a sensual kiss on his lips. Blake slid his tongue over Alex's, gliding over his soft palate, searching out every corner of his mouth. He moved inside Alex, pushing in even farther then slowly retreating until his cockhead was almost at the rim, before pressing back in, harder this time, faster.

Alex keened and arched upward, once again, holding Blake tight inside himself. Blake changed the angle of entry so he could nail Alex's prostate with each pass and he rammed in harder, urged on by Alex's moans and whimpers filled with lust and need. Spurts of pre-cum coated Alex's torso and the onset of the orgasm Blake had subdued, returned full force.

He gripped Alex's swollen shaft and pumped it, matching the rhythm of his hard thrusts. Alex dug his fingers into Blake's shoulders, shuddering under him, crying out his name as he came.

Blake couldn't hold back any longer, and now that Alex had found his release, there was no need. He groaned, every nerve ending in his body seeming to hum and spark, the hot rush of his cum filling Alex when he spiraled out of control into a blissful oblivion.

They lay wrapped in each other's arms trading soft kisses until Alex stirred. "Oh, wow…" Alex's lips on his ear made Blake shiver. "I love feeling you come inside me. I didn't think making love with you could get any better, but each time I'm wrong about that. You are amazing."

Blake smiled and kissed the tip of Alex's nose. "You have something to do with that too, you know. We just fit together so well."

"True that."

"How was Oliver since he got laid?"

Alex laughed. "I haven't seen him, but he'll be there tomorrow night. I guess his Dom is keeping him busy."

"I can't wait to meet this guy. Color me intrigued."

* * * *

The following day they played tourist, using a hop-on-hop-off bus to visit some of the sights Blake hadn't yet seen, then ending up at Fisherman's Wharf for a late lunch.

Doreen was waiting for them when they got to the gallery. Alex hadn't said anything to her about Oliver and Dominic, but as it turned out, there was no need. Oliver's fawning over his Dom when he'd introduced them had been evidence enough. Doreen rolled her eyes at Alex and Blake while she related the story.

"The poor kid doesn't know what he's letting himself in for," she said without much sympathy.

"I have a feeling it might be the other way around," Alex told her.

"Oh, do tell." Doreen had to wait for the explanation as Oliver bore down on them at that moment, all smiles.

Blake winced at the man's forced ebullience. *What a phony… If he tries to put a hug on me, I might throw up. Smarmy doesn't even begin to describe this guy.*

Oliver drew the slight young man who'd been following him into the group. "Dominic, you've met Alex and Doreen, and this is Blake, Alex's *boyfriend.*"

"Nice to meet you." Blake held out his hand and it was taken timidly with a shy smile. *Can this really be the Dom Alex was talking about?*

Any further conversation was put on hold when several people entered the gallery and Alex, Doreen and Oliver went to greet them, Oliver dragging Dominic with him. Left on his own, Blake wandered over to the bar and ordered a glass of chardonnay. He leaned against the bar and sipped his drink, watching Alex schmooze with an elderly couple who seemed very much enamored of Alex's work, or Alex himself. He couldn't blame them for either one.

Alex's smile really did light up a room, and what Blake loved about that smile was that it was genuine. Considering everything Alex had been through, it was amazing that he had not turned out to have a bitter soul. But Blake knew that was not him at all. Every moment spent with Alex convinced Blake of the love he had for life and for his craft, and now for Blake too.

It was selfish of him he knew, but he couldn't wait to drag him out of here, away from those who were occupying his time. *Instead of leaving him all to me.* Yeah, he was being selfish, but he loved him so, everything about him, every part of him, and yes, when he asked again, Blake was going to say yes to living with him. In the eyes of some, it might be too soon, but Blake knew it to be right, and Alex did too. *And that's all that matters, yes? Yes.*

His heart quickened when Alex crossed the gallery floor toward him. "You all right there all by yourself? I'm sorry, it's busier that I thought it would be."

"I'm fine, babe. Enjoying the scenery, if you must know."

"Oh, who's here?" he asked, looking around.

"You, lover. The one man in this gallery I have eyes for."

"That's sweet. You want to leave?"

"You can't."

"I know." His eyes flashed with mischief. "But if you threw me over your shoulder and made a run for it, I wouldn't holler too loud."

"I love you." Blake leaned forward and brushed a kiss over Alex's warm lips. "Oh, so much."

"Hold that thought," Alex whispered. "And never forget it."

"Impossible."

* * * *

Monday morning, and Blake sighed as he stared around him at his grim surroundings. *So many unhappy people, brought here by cruel circumstances.* And it was his job to make sure that he could at least set some of it right. Unfortunately, sometimes the judge didn't agree, and appeals weren't always a sure thing. *But let's not go down that path.*

From what he'd read of the case he was representing, it sounded open-and-shut. An abusive father and husband. Both wife and daughter claiming sexual, physical and verbal abuse, and they had the evidence to prove it.

The husband had been arrested, and Blake's heart broke for the little girl when she cowered at the sight of her father now shackled but with a murderous gaze fixed on them both. The defense struggled to make a case, and Blake could tell the judge was anything but impressed. All that was left for Blake to do was state the facts and present the evidence. This was a bench trial, and without a jury, there was no need for emotional cries for justice. The facts spoke for themselves, and the arresting officers testified to the gross state of the home, the drug use by the father, followed by statements made by medical personnel. However, Blake couldn't resist emphasizing the husband's vileness for the judge's benefit.

Normally, sentencing was reserved for a future date, but after the judge spoke to the defendant and received sneering one-word answers, he said he could see no reason to delay. Afterward, Blake spoke with the mother and daughter and the social services people who were now charged with the family's care. He assured the daughter who trembled in his arms when he hugged her that she had nothing more to be terrified of. The man who had terrorized her would be gone for a long time. He left the courtroom and was pleased to see Keren talking with a small group of women. She waved when she saw him then, after excusing herself, she walked over to where he waited.

"Hi, Keren, how are you?"

"Okay. Just giving some new recruits a tour of the courthouse. How are you?"

"Good, thanks. May I ask how Joey's enjoying his new home?"

Keren sighed. "I wish I had better news for you. Trudy's at her wits' end trying to cope with his moods." She met his worried expression with one of her own. "I don't want to interfere, but the good match I thought it would be just isn't working. She and Bill don't want to give up on him, but it's hard on them, and poor Joey. I've asked them to give it another few weeks to see if he settles in better."

"I'm sorry to hear that. I was hoping a safe and comfortable environment would be the answer after the rotten situation he was in before."

"You and me both. Well..." She looked over at her group. "I better get back." She paused and touched Blake's arm. "I'll let you know how things turn out."

"Thanks. I wish I could say I'd help, but I don't think that would be a good idea."

Keren looked away. "Maybe, I don't know. Bye for now."

He watched her walk away and felt bad for the Davises, and, of course, for Joey. Darn it, but he'd hoped this would work out for him. And it might yet. Maybe he just needed some more time to adjust. Keren had mentioned Joey's moods being a problem. That was surprising. Granted, he hadn't spent weeks with Joey, but if anything, moody was not a word he'd use to describe the little guy.

He called Alex when he got back to his office. "Hi, how's your day so far?"

"Okay, missing you, but what's new about that? How'd your case go?"

"Good, at least for the wife and daughter. For the husband, not so much. He's gone for a long time. So, I saw Keren on my way out of the courthouse."

"Oh yeah? How is she?"

"She told me Joey's not happy in his foster home."

"Oh no, that's too bad. Is there something you can do?"

"I have a feeling it would be regarded as interfering." Blake sighed. "From what Keren said, Trudy Davis is finding it hard to deal with Joey's moodiness. Keren didn't say Trudy was ready to send Joey back, but she did say it didn't seem to be the good match she envisaged."

"You did send in your application to be a foster parent, right?"

"Yes."

"Well, can't you maybe put the word out that you're available should the Davises decide to send Joey back?"

"No, it doesn't work that way, Alex. And like I said, it could be construed as interference on my part. It may all work out in the end. I'm sure Trudy and Bill are showing Joey he's welcome in their home and giving him affection. It's what he needs, Alex."

"It's what he'd get from you, Blake. You'd be such a good dad. I know you would."

Despite Alex's words of encouragement, Blake found it hard to shake the feeling of depression that settled over him for the rest of the day. He tried to imagine Joey being moody and ungrateful for what Trudy and Bill were doing for him, and it just didn't compute.

He's such a loving kid, so eager to explore and enjoy new things. He had no way of knowing what his foster parents' home environment might be like, but he was certain Keren wouldn't have put Joey in a place where he would feel alienated and unhappy. Too bad Blake couldn't go over there and talk to him. Blake remembered Joey being pretty attentive when they were together, listening to his stories, happy to stay close by his side and not run off on his own. A good kid. *So what's gone wrong?*

* * * *

Alex was bummed that Keren had given Blake such unsettling news about Joey being unhappy with his new foster home. Even when Blake had tried to sound optimistic about maybe Joey settling down over time, the sadness had come through in his inflections. Alex didn't know Joey that well, having spent only a few hours with him, but he'd seemed such a happy-go-lucky kid, and it was obvious he'd adored Blake. And therein perhaps lay the problem. Perhaps Joey had been fixated on Blake becoming his dad.

His cell vibrated on the hotel room desk, and he glanced at the number, not recognizing it. "Alexander Martin."

"Oh, it's *Alexander* now, is it? I suppose it's better than the sissy *Alex* you used to call yourself."

"Who the hell is this?" Even as he asked, a shiver of revulsion coasted down his spine.

"It's your father, that's who the hell it is."

"Why?"

"What d'you mean why?"

"Why are you calling me?"

"Because I'm your father. Isn't that enough reason to call you?"

"No, actually it's not. Not after twenty years of silence. Not after you sent me to some hellhole for five fucking years, *Father*! No, it isn't reason enough." Alex told himself not to lose it, not to let the old fuck know he had him riled up, not to let him have that kind of satisfaction. "What d'you want?"

"An apology."

"You must be joking. An apology? That's what you owe *me*. What in hell could I have to apologize to you for?"

"For not coming to your mother's funeral. For not having the decency to say goodbye and tell her you're sorry for the sins you brought upon our house."

"Jesus, you sound like a bad biblical movie starring Kirk Cameron. Listen to me, *Pops*. I don't know how you got my number, but do me a favor and throw it away. Twenty years ago you disowned me, had me locked up in a place where I thought about killing myself. In all those years you never once wrote to me, asked me if I was well, never visited me like loving parents do. In those years I learned to hate you, and the woman who called herself my mother. Aunt Katherine was more like a mother to me, the one person in our family who gave a shit about whether I lived or died. Not you, and certainly not the creeps you forced me to live with, be tortured by, humiliated by. Oh listen, you've got me on a roll now. Like me to go on? 'Cause I've got a ton more to lay on your miserable ass!"

"You always were an abomination. You—"

"Shut up, old man. If anyone is an abomination, it's you. You were an abominable father. You professed to be a man of God, but you couldn't have been further from that than the Devil himself. And here's the clincher, Dad—I'm still gay, and guess who my boyfriend is, the man I love more than life itself? Blake Carson! Right, even *you* couldn't kill the love we had for each other, and now have for each other all over again. How'd you like those apples, eh? All that money you spent trying to change me into someone I could never be, because I was born this way. You get it? Your God made me who I am, so get over it. And don't you dare ever call me again."

"You sodomite, I'll ruin you!" his father screeched.

"Oh yeah? And how are you gonna do that exactly?"

"I hear you're somebody now, *famous*. If taking pictures of sodomites can be called being famous." His father's voice was loaded with malice. "Well, how would you like it if I let it be known what you are—a stinking homosexual!"

Alex snorted. "I've got news for you, old man. This ain't the Dark Ages anymore, and I'm not a kid anymore to be bullied by the likes of you. It's not illegal to be gay. You might consider it immoral, but that's your cross to bear, and I can assure you it won't shock anyone who knows me, or my work. So, what else you got?"

"You are going to hell and —"

Alex disconnected the call. *Oh, my freaking God!* Now when he thought about it, why did he hang up? He could have gone on for a helluva lot longer, vilifying the old goat, tearing him a new one, over and over. But enough is enough, and after that conversation, he didn't think he could stand listening to that carping voice for one more minute.

In twenty years, nothing had changed. He was still the same hate-filled sanctimonious bigot who had judged Alex unfit to live under his roof. He'd already been fifty when Alex had been born. A *mistake* he'd told his son, who hadn't fully understood what he'd meant at the time. A mistake he couldn't wait to get rid of. Despite everything, Alex couldn't quite stop the rush of tears that filled his eyes. Not for his parents — he'd never cry for them. But when he thought of the love Blake's parents had shown for their son, and the affection they'd not held back on for Alex, he remembered wishing over and over that they'd been his parents too. That he could have grown up in a loving atmosphere full of hugs and words of praise.

He managed a rueful smile. Blake being his brother would certainly have changed the dynamics of their relationship. Instead, he had the best friend in all the world and now they'd found each other again, and nothing Harold Martin could do or say would destroy that. The bastard could fester in his hatred for the rest of his rotten life, and Alex could think of no better end for him.

He wiped at his eyes with the palms of his hands. No, he would not give in to the despair that threatened to overwhelm him. He was stronger than that and with Blake by his side, he knew he could overcome any vestiges of PTSD that might have been lurking waiting for something like this to trigger a relapse. Well, that wasn't going to happen!

This week couldn't end fast enough. He wanted to be back in LA in Blake's arms, kissing him, holding him, being fucked by him over and over. And he better have decided about them moving in together. He wasn't going to take anything else but yes for an answer!

Chapter Nineteen

Most of Blake's week had been taken up with financial committee meetings in San Diego. He'd opted to drive instead of staying over in the city which, he later mused, freeway traffic being what it was, probably wasn't the brightest decision. The worst part was that the meetings had extended into the weekend when Alex would be finishing up his exhibition in San Francisco. He'd wanted to be there, but he'd had to cancel at the last minute.

"But I'll be at the airport to meet you on Sunday," he'd told his lover, hating the piss-poor consolation he was offering.

"That's okay, babe," Alex had assured him, *"I'll be busy getting everything packed up and on the truck, headed for storage. My plane won't get in until seven p.m."*

"You'll be too exhausted for me to have my way with you," Blake had complained.

"Never too exhausted for that, lover."

In the car coming back from LAX, Alex told Blake he'd had a call from his father.

"Wow, that can't have been pleasant," Blake remarked.

"I think it was less pleasant for him by the time I was finished."

"Got a lot off your chest then?"

"You could say that, but he only heard a fraction of what I really should've laid on him. He wanted me to apologize for not showing up at my mother's funeral."

Blake bit his lip but didn't say anything.

"I'm not the bad guy, am I, Blake?" Alex rubbed Blake's thigh as if searching for comfort.

Blake wished they weren't in the car so he could take Alex in his arms, but he sure as hell could tell him. "You most definitely are not the bad guy, sweetheart." He covered Alex's hand with his, squeezing it gently. "You are a brave and gentle soul who deserved so much better in life. Better parents for a start. A mom and dad who treasured you and saw the goodness in you just like I did, and still do. I'm sorry you had to deal with his calling you."

"I told him that you and I were together again."

"Ah, that must've gone over well."

"It sure as hell gave me the most pleasure. He threatened to ruin me by telling everyone I was, and I quote, 'a stinking homosexual'."

"Jesus, Alex. What a god-awful person he is. I hope you told him that wouldn't exactly come as a big surprise to most people."

"I did, then I hung up. It would've been pointless in prolonging the conversation."

"When we get back to your place, remind me I owe you one."

Alex turned to him, surprised. "You owe me one what?"

"The biggest, most comforting hug you've ever had in your life. I just want to wrap you up in my arms and hold you until the pain goes away."

Alex laid his head on Blake's shoulder and hugged his arm. "I love you so much."

"And I love you so much, too."

Tired as Alex was, Blake's comforting hug turned into so much more, and they spent the night and long hours of the morning making love. Having Blake sink inside him, joined to him as if they were one being, was for Alex, the true remedy for all that ailed him. Assholes like Oliver, rabid bigots like his father, all faded from his consciousness and he allowed a peaceful, dreamless sleep to take over.

They'd slept until Blake was late for work and had to dash like a madman around Alex's apartment getting ready, much to Alex's amusement.

"Wouldn't you know I've got one of those meetings again today," Blake complained as he hopped about, trying to get a leg inside his pants. "The last one for the quarter, thank goodness, and thankfully it's here in LA, not San Diego. Anyway, I'll check in with you later."

Alex rolled off the bed and padded over to him, pressing his naked body against him. "I'll miss you."

Blake kissed him. "Same. I love you."

"Love you too. I'll fix us dinner tonight here."

"That's why I love you. Bye."

* * * *

The meeting proved to be even more boring than the ones in San Diego. Blake knew they were necessary evils. The company had to stay afloat, and a lot of their funding came from grants and donors, most of their cases being pro bono. Still, couldn't they liven it up a bit? The accountants' droning on about statistics and figures were lulling him to sleep. He really hadn't had enough last night, or this morning. Sleep, that was. But that was all good.

It was great having Alex back. In between making love, they'd talked about the future, and Blake had agreed to move in with Alex. He had to give a month's notice at his place, but in the back of his mind he was okay with that. It gave Alex time to change his mind if he started to get cold feet. After all, as he'd pointed out, they'd only been dating for seven weeks and maybe there were habits of Blake's that Alex would find annoying. And then what?

He'd received a slap on his chest for that remark and a reminder that it might only have been seven weeks but what about the year before Alex had been sent away, and all the years when they had never forgotten about each other? Alex's look of determination had helped Blake put aside his anxiety that things could go wrong between them.

"*Impossible,*" Alex had told him, trailing kisses over his jaw and throat and making it difficult for Blake to hold on to a coherent thought other than the urge to ravish the man in his arms again, and again.

His cell vibrating in his pants pocket made him jump. He took a surreptitious peek at the screen and frowned. *Keren. Wonder what she wants?* He had to let the call go to message. Roger would want to talk about the meeting afterward, so he'd better listen up. Nevertheless, he worried that it might be more bad news about Joey. He listened while Roger talked about a gala evening to raise funds for charities and a pitch for donors to help keep Benson and Sellers afloat.

After the meeting, while they were all filing out of the room, he remembered Keren's call and checked for a message.

"Hi, Blake, Trudy called me this morning really agitated. Call me back when you can."

Okay, this was for certain a Joey problem, but what could he do about it? He wanted what was best for the kid but getting involved other than in a legal capacity might cause more problems. He punched in her number. "Hi, Keren, what's going on?"

"Blake, I'm so sorry to involve you in this, but Trudy and Bill have taken Joey back to the care center. Trudy was in tears, but she just can't stand seeing him so sad. She said perhaps someone else can make him smile."

Oh boy. "I'm sorry it didn't work out. The Davises seemed like nice people. Tell them not to give up on finding the right kid."

"What about you, Blake? Joey was so fond of you. Have you thought of fostering?"

"I have, but it's complicated."

"Well, maybe you could go see him at the center. I know Estelle wouldn't mind."

"I'll talk to the boss, see if I can get the afternoon off to go over there."

After he'd hung up, he walked over to Roger's office and tapped on the doorframe. "You have a minute?"

"Yes, come on in, Blake. What's up?"

Blake sat and explained the situation with Joey and the Davises. "You might remember he was an abused kid along with two little girls fostered by a couple, name of Harris. We had the case. Clive got in an accident, and I took it over."

"Oh yes, I remember."

"Anyway, Joey's new foster home hasn't worked out. They took him back to the center, and Keren from social services asked if maybe I could go over to see him. He seemed to take a shine to me, so maybe I could cheer him up."

Roger gazed at him for a long moment before he said, "Have you thought of fostering, Blake? If the kid's comfortable around you, maybe you're the answer he needs."

"Yeah, but you really can't pick the kid you want from the system, and it can take weeks to get licensed. Plus Alex, my boyfriend, and I are kind of in a new relationship, although he was open to maybe having a kid, but that can take months, and right now, Joey needs a home where he'll feel safe and loved, and—"

"What about legal guardianship?" Roger said. "We can have the forms filled out here, get a court date. I can pull a few strings there, so we don't have to wait weeks. Maybe days—if that even. If it works out with you, Alex and the boy, you could think of starting the adoption process down the road."

Blake stared at Roger, his mouth slightly open. "Why didn't I think of that? Legal guardianship, I mean."

Roger smiled. "I don't know, why didn't you?"

"Wow, thanks, Roger. If you can help get me a court date soon, that would be terrific."

"I'll get right on it. You'll need some good references, but I don't think that's a problem. You have me for a start, and the entire office!"

Blake called Alex on the way over to the center. "Are you busy right now?"

"I'm over at the storage depot, but almost finished. You need something?"

"Can you meet me over at the care center? I'm going to see Joey. It's a long story, well not really, but I'll explain more later. If you can meet me there, it would be great."

"Then I'll meet you there. Love you, babe."

"Love you too. More and more every day."

* * * *

Estelle's face lit up when she opened the door and saw Blake there. "Oh, Mr. Carson, what a pleasure. I was prayin' you'd come by. He's in the break room with Spencer, but even he can't get much outta him. And he's just a big kid himself!"

"Good to see you, Estelle. I might have the answer to our problem, but I have to talk to Joey first. My boyfriend, Alex, should be right behind me, so let him in, will you?"

"That handsome fella? You bet I'll let him in. Joey, look who's here to see you."

Spencer grinned at him, but when Joey's lackluster gaze fell on Blake, his eyes grew wide, and he burst into tears.

Well, not the reception I was hoping for. "Joey..." Blake knelt in front of him and smiled sadly. "You not pleased to see me?"

Joey slipped off the stool he'd been sitting on and ran into Blake's open arms. He hiccupped through his tears. "You'll leave me again."

"No, no." Blake gathered him against his chest and stood. "How would you like it if you came to live with me and my friend, Alex? You remember him? We went to the park, to the swings, and he bought us some ice cream."

"You won't leave again?"

"Never. Well, only when I have to go to work, but I'll be with you every morning and every night, and in between times—"

"I'll be there," Alex said from behind them. He took Joe's tiny hand in his. "I'm Alex."

"Arex," Joey said solemnly. "Ice cweam man."

"That's right. We could go get some right now if you like."

"How about it, Estelle?" Blake stroked Joey's soft dark hair. "We'll bring some back for you and Spencer if you like."

"That'd be swell. But first you have to tell me what you have planned here."

"Something I should've thought of by myself earlier. Legal guardianship."

Estelle planted her hands on her hips. "You so should have. And you an attorney an' all."

"It'll take a few days, but we'll come by and see Joey every day till it's settled."

"Hey, that sounds cool," Spencer said. "Weren't you sayin' something about ice cream? Also cool."

"That's right." Estelle waved at them "Off you go and bring me back some chocolate ice cream."

"I'll have raspberry," Spencer said, "in a cone."

They set off toward the park, Joey holding tight to Blake's and Alex's hands as he skipped along between them.

Alex smiled at Blake. "Well, this is a much better day than yesterday, right?"

"Well…" He winked at Alex. "Apart from you know what."

Joey tugged on his hand. "What you know what?"

Alex laughed. "Little ears hear an awful lot, you know."

Blake groaned. "We have to get a bigger place."

E p i l o g u e

Six months later

When did we turn into party animals? Blake wondered after he'd picked up the cake for the gathering later that afternoon. Since he'd moved in with Alex, and since he'd become Joey's legal guardian, it seemed they'd had more parties in six months than Blake could remember since he'd been a kid. He'd loved parties then, and he wanted Joey to know the joy of being the center of attention, surrounded by friends who made him feel special and loved.

Today was Joey's fifth birthday and it was a kind of a double celebration. Three days ago, Blake and Alex had become the adoptive parents of Joey Carmichael. They hadn't told him yet, but had the certificate of adoption framed, ready to present it to him for his birthday.

A text from Alex. *You got the cake?*

What cake?

What d'you mean what cake? THE cake!

Oh, that cake. You get the balloons?

How can I get the balloons? Joey's with me.

Guess I better do it then.

You were supposed to do it and have them and the cake home when we get there.

That's right, I was.

Blake!

Keep a lid on it. I'm home and everything's copacetic.

Oh.

Say thank you, Blake.

Thank you, Blake.

That'll do for the time being, but later, oh boy.

Winking emoji. I hear ya. Later, babe.

Blake had been put in charge of decorating, which was pretty easy as it entailed mostly balloons and streamers, and in no time he had the place looking festive, if he said so himself. They had invited Doreen of course, Patrick and Mark, his friends from his internship days and Dale and Henry who, over the last six months, had become good friends, Estelle and Spencer, Keren, Roger and his wife Maureen and the

Fuller family that included Loren and Emily, Joey's friends from his fostered days.

As he trailed some glittering streamers across the sideboard in the dining area, his gaze fell on two framed photos. One, the selfie of Alex and him taken that day in the park early on in their renewed relationship, and one with Joey perched between them on the couch, the first day they'd moved in together. Joey's smile was so big it took up his entire face. Blake couldn't stop the tears that sprang to his eyes when he remembered that day and the knowledge that he and Alex were the reasons for that amazing smile. Joey at last had what he'd needed all his young life. A loving family and friends who showered him with affection, and though they'd deny it, spoiled him just a little.

Sounds of the door opening and voices, one a melodious tenor and one more like a reed pipe yelling "We're ho-ome" left no doubt who was indeed home. He knelt down to catch the little whirlwind that flew into his arms and covered his face with wet kisses. Blake hoisted Joey onto his shoulder and watched his eyes grow huge when he spied all the balloons and colored glitter hanging from the ceiling.

"Party!" he cried, and Blake lifted him so he could bat at one of the balloons.

"Yes, another one." He smiled at Alex. "I was trying to figure out how many we've had in the last six months. Seems like a lot."

"Well…" Alex counted on his fingers. "There was the one we gave when you became Joey's legal guardian, then there was Thanksgiving, Christmas, New Years, our wedding on Valentine's Day, my birthday in March and now Joey's."

"Daddy have birthday?" Joey asked, rearranging Blake's curls with his tiny fingers. He had started calling Blake Daddy within weeks of living with them, and Alex, Dada. Because they'd known almost from the beginning that they would adopt Joey, they had answered to the names right away.

"Better enjoy it while we can," Alex had said wryly. "When he grows up it'll be 'old man' or 'hey you'."

"Yes, Daddy has a birthday. It's in August, and we'll have another party."

"With bawoons?"

"Yes, with bawoons." He lowered Joey to the floor and sat beside him. Alex picked up the framed adoption certificate and came to sit with them.

"We have something special to show you, Joey," he said, giving him a kiss on the cheek. He held up the frame for Joey to see. Joey screwed up his eyes then touched the glass.

"It says that Blake and Alexander Carson-Martin are now the proud daddies of Joey Carmichael…soon to be Joey Carson-Martin. You are our son, Joey. Is that okay?" Joey looked at Alex then at Blake, and Blake could see in his expression the dawning of a realization of what that meant to him.

"Twuly?" His eyes were brimming with tears, and Blake had to swipe at his own eyes to stop the moisture from trickling down his face. He gazed at Alex who was making no effort to stop his tears.

"Yes, truly, Joey. You are Daddy's and Dada's son now and forever. Big hug now. Happy Birthday, Joey." Blake put an arm around Alex and one around Joey and held them tight. "Love you both."

They were quiet, their only sounds sighs and a lot of sniffling as they clung together. A sharp knock at the door had them scrambling to their feet.

"Oh my God," Alex muttered, "I must look a wreck. Stall everybody while I go wash my face."

"You look fine." He ran his thumb over Alex's cheekbones. "There, good as new." He kissed Alex's lips. "Love you."

"Love you too."

"Daddy, Dada…" Joey had opened the door. "Auntie Doween's here."

Blake smacked Alex's ass. "Okay, Mr. Unforgettable—let the party begin!"

Want to see more from this author? Here's a taster for you to enjoy!

The Love Between Us
J.P. Bowie

Excerpt

From his position behind the bar at Bobby's Tavern, Matt Johnson surveyed the crowd that filled almost every square inch of the largest gay bar in San Diego. He sighed. Another night of forcing a smile to his lips and thinking of something humorous to pass on to the customers who got tipsier, and sometimes downright drunkier, with every passing hour.

It wasn't as if he didn't like his job — he did — but in the past few months, he'd felt as if, somehow, he'd been left behind. Not sexually, for sure. He had more than his fair share of guys wanting to spend time with a hot bartender. Matt knew he was hot — he'd been told so many, many times — but, it seemed, not hot enough to keep a guy interested for more than a few nights. He was still young, he'd told himself a hundred times. There were still a lot of years ahead for him to find the 'one', weren't there?

It was just that in the four years he'd been working at Bobby's Tavern, almost everyone he'd known, whether they worked together or were friends he'd see on his nights off, had somehow managed to get themselves seriously involved with another guy. So, why couldn't he? Was he regarded as that much of a flake? He'd overheard a remark like that a few months ago, from someone who thought he knew him, and Matt had wanted to turn around and say, "You don't know me at all." But he hadn't said it, couldn't really, because the man was a customer, and rudeness from the bar staff was not allowed at Bobby's Tavern.

Jack Felton, the owner and manager, had fired a couple of bartenders for just that offense, and if there was something Matt needed badly, it was to keep this job. Nowhere else, without a college degree, could he earn the kind of money he did here. Steve, his relief bartender, was studying to be an environmental engineer. Well, good luck to him, but he was going to miss the tips that didn't come with a job like that. Still, he did have that hunk of a wealthy boyfriend he was living with should things not pan out for him.

Matt sighed again then had to quickly jump to it as Brett, the other bartender on duty, looked like he was getting swamped with orders all of a sudden.

"What'll it be?" he asked a cute, fresh-faced blond kid who yelled his order over the combined din of voices and music that was a nightly staple at Bobby's.

"Two screwdrivers and a Stella."

Is this kid twenty-one? "You have ID?"

The 'kid' laughed, his gaze settling on Matt's bare chest. "I'm twenty-three, but thanks for the compliment." He handed over his driver's license without hesitation.

Matt smiled after he'd glanced at it. "You must get that a lot...Taylor."

"I do...uh, what's your name?"

"Matt."

"Nice to meet you, Matt. Anyway, I get asked for ID nearly every time in bars me and my buds don't go to a lot. We live in LA and usually go to Sykes on Melrose.

They know us there." He waved a hand behind him to include the two guys standing there. Both looked to be the same age as Taylor.

"Well, enjoy your evening," Matt said while he fixed their drinks.

"We're here for the weekend, so we'll most likely come here again." Taylor gave him a flirty smile. "Are you working tomorrow night?"

Matt nodded and passed Taylor the two screwdrivers. "The Stella for you?"

"Yes." Taylor turned to hand over the screwdrivers to his friends. When he turned back to face Matt, he asked, "What time d'you get off tonight?"

"Not till two a.m., sorry." He watched the frown of disappointment crease Taylor's forehead. "But I'm off at nine tomorrow night if you're thinking of buying me a drink."

Taylor's expression lightened. "That, and anything else you'd like."

"It's a date. That'll be fifteen for the screwdrivers. Your beer's on the house."

"Thanks." He slipped Matt a twenty. "Keep the change."

"Lose your friends tomorrow night. They won't be hurt, will they?"

"They're married, so, no." Taylor grinned at him. "They'll be in bed by nine." He stepped out of the way to let another couple of customers reach the bar. "See you later, Matt."

He should have felt better about scoring with the cute guy, but if the truth be told, Matt was getting tired of the one-night stands, tired of the indifference after the second or third night. He'd always said he was happy to be some guy's fuck buddy, happy for there to be no real commitment, just good times. If the sex was really good, then so much the better. But recently it had definitely palled when he thought about what some people he knew had…the same man in their bed every night, and delight with the status quo.

Taylor came back to the bar, three or four more times, his smile of anticipation always in place. *Seems like a nice guy*, Matt thought. *Too bad he lives in LA, land of the parking lot freeways.* Toward the end of the evening, he scanned the thinning crowd to see if Taylor had hung around, but there was no sign of him or his friends. *That's okay, I'm bushed anyway.* Friday and Saturday nights were always a bear, but the tips made it all worthwhile.

On his way home, he stopped in at Fawkes, an all-night café a few blocks from his apartment. Not the chicest place in town, but the burgers were to die for, and Matt was starving. While he waited for his burger to go, Matt stared out of the window at the late-night stragglers wending their ways either home or to a local hotel. Mostly guys, their arms around each other probably for support, he reckoned, rather than affection, although it could have been a combination of the two.

Anyway, it's more than I have right now. Okay, he had to stop with the self-pity. It wasn't attractive and nobody had the patience to listen to a whiner. Nobody he knew, at any rate.

"Here you go, Matt," Al, the guy in charge at night said. "I put some fries on the side even though you didn't ask for 'em." He stared at Matt's flat stomach. "You gotta lotta room for 'em, by the looks of you."

"Thanks, Al." He'd been coming to Fawkes off and on for the last couple of years, so he knew better than to argue about the fries. He didn't have to eat them when he got home. Tonight, he just might. Burger, fries and a beer. *Better than… Nah, not really.*

Working at Bobby's, he was able to afford a nice apartment. *As nice as Jason's, anyway,* he thought, looking around at the cozy living room. But Jason had moved into that fancy place with David, the guy he'd met at the gym. *Stole him right from under my nose.* Not really, but it had rankled for a bit. He and Jason had been fuck buddies, although if he were being honest with himself, he wished he'd asked for more. He didn't see Jason often these days, like he used to. Guys who got serious usually didn't make a habit of frequenting gay bars, apart from getting together with friends occasionally. Matt guessed he could understand that. Once a guy was hooked, there wasn't that pressing need to go out and mingle with other 'desperately seeking someones'.

Man, but he was getting jaundiced in his opinions. When had that happened? He wasn't desperate…he had his share of the good life. And tomorrow night there'd be one more slice — Taylor, all hot and ready to get fucked before he had to go back to La-la land.

He stripped, threw his clothes in the laundry basket then slipped on a pair of shorts and, after getting a can of beer from the fridge, prepared to devour the burger and fries. He turned on the television, mainly to fill the room with sound instead of the silence that seemed to pervade the space on the nights he came home alone.

But I'm not lonely…not really. I have friends. Brett and Steve at Bobby's…Jason. Yes, he's still a friend of mine. We were real close there for a while until…but I still see him now and then, don't I? When he comes in with his buddies, he always stops and says hello.

"Fuck it." He stood and walked into the kitchen to dump the burger wrappers and get himself another beer. Truth was, he missed the times he'd spent with Jason. He'd been so sweet in bed. Sweet and kinda rough sometimes. He'd liked to mix it up. Matt had liked that too, but Jason had never made him feel he was just there for the sex. Afterward they'd cuddled and talked...almost like boyfriends.

There had been others since then, maybe too many others, and none of them had made him feel like Jason had. Well, he'd messed up for sure, letting him slip away like that without telling him, without saying the words that might have kept him by Matt's side.

"I love you." Yeah, those were the words. The words he hadn't said, had never said to another guy...and now it was too late. Jason and David had been living together now for six months, and from what he'd heard it didn't sound like they were having any problems or regrets. Not that he'd wish them to have. *I'm not that fucking desperate...*

* * * *

Saturday night and the place was jumping. It was difficult to tell which was louder—the clamor of the crowd or the blare of the pop-rock reverberating through the speakers. Another night when Matt would go home with his ears still ringing. Steve had called to say he was going to be late and hoped Matt didn't mind. Yes, Matt minded. He'd told Taylor he'd be off at nine, and he couldn't leave Brett on his own, not on a night like this. They'd even got the bar waiters mixing drinks to help them out.

"Fuckin' Steve," he growled under his breath. He was probably late because he was banging Eric through the mattress. He told himself he wasn't annoyed because he was jealous. He got plenty of action—and probably would tonight—but it irked him that Steve thought it was okay to call at the last minute and say he'd be late. He scanned the crowd to see if Taylor was already among the throng so he could tell him he'd be late getting off shift, but so far there was no sign of the cute blond.

For the next half-hour or so he was kept busy mixing drinks and pulling pints, and when Steve arrived and apologized again for being late, he was surprised to see it was already nine-thirty. And still no sign of Taylor. For a moment Matt couldn't believe the guy would be a no-show. That didn't happen very often. In fact, he couldn't remember the last time he'd been stood up. Maybe he'd got sick or run out of money and had to go home, or…he'd gotten lucky with someone else.

"So, are you leaving?" Steve asked. "Or are you so enamored of working here you wanna stay till closing time?"

"I'm leaving. How's Eric?" Matt scanned the crowd again—still no sign of his supposed date.

"Delightful as always," Steve said smugly. "I can't believe it's been nearly nine months already. We had dinner over at Jason and David's place last night. Jason said to tell you 'hi'."

"Did he?" Matt tried not to feel hurt. He really did, but it didn't work too well. Jason had never asked him over for dinner, but maybe that was David's decision. Most likely Jason had told him about their fuck-buddy days and the guy maybe thought he didn't need any more competition. Jason was a looker, and although David was handsome and all, he was older and… *Christ, I am being such a prick right now.*

"You okay?" Steve squeezed Matt's shoulder. "You look like you're in pain."

"No, I'm okay. Just wonderin' if I'll go home or take in a movie. I've had enough of bars for the night."

Steve nodded. "Know what you mean. When I get off shift, I am so ready just to get home to my man." He flinched. "Yeah, sorry, Matt, didn't mean to sound smug." Matt had confided in Steve a while back that he and Jason had a sexual relationship and how he, Matt, had wished it could have been more. Steve had sympathized but hadn't come up with any advice, but by then of course, David had come along and that, as they say, was that.

Matt forced out a laugh. "Hey, some of us prefer to be single-o. No ball and chain for me, not yet anyway. Okay, I'll see you tomorrow…if you can pull yourself away from your *man*."

He went into the back room to get his shirt and slip it on then walked through the bar, looking for any sign of the missing Taylor. By the time he got to the exit, he'd been groped about a dozen times. *Nothing like drunken queens to forget their manners.* He said hi to a couple of familiar faces then walked past the smokers outside and headed for his car and home.

About the Author

J.P. Bowie was born in Scotland and toured British theatres in numerous musical shows including Stephen Sondheim's Company.

He emigrated to the States and worked in Las Vegas, Nevada for the magicians Siegfried and Roy as their Head of Wardrobe at the Mirage Hotel. He is currently living with his husband in sunny San Diego, California.

J.P. Bowie loves to hear from readers. You can find his contact information, website details and author profile page at https://www.pride-publishing.com

PUBLISHING

Sign up for our newsletter and find out about all our romance book releases, eBook sales and promotions, sneak peeks and FREE romance books!